CW00972738

Where the Swallows Fly

Anthony James

ISBN: 979864432793

Disclaimer: This work is a work of fiction and any reference to persons living or dead is purely accidental.

Thanks to my wife Dawn for her patient support.

Chapter 1

The beginning: – John Betts.

I know I'm coming to the end, because I'm not thinking about sex all the time. In fact, I don't think about it, sex that is, at all anymore. Maybe I think that I miss it, the urge, the anxiety, the application, the dream. It's definitely something that is no longer here. There's no oil in the sump of this old wreck. That's why I know this is the beginning of my end. Since I was fourteen, seventy years ago, I've lived with it and now I miss the constant itching urge in my pants, and that's a fact.

It's warm and my bed is comfortable, but this is not my home. It's the home, a home for old buggers who live here until they go out in a bag. Don't get me wrong, they're really nice here, they look after me and will even help me undress if I let them. Of course, I don't, that would be tempting fate.

This House is in a decaying avenue in a miserable town. Well, perhaps not all that miserable, there is something graceful about the decaying Georgian crescent that sweeps down the hill to 'Swallow House' I'm not sure what kind of Swallow the man had in mind but it certainly swallows up the inmates. The house once stood in the countryside and it still has a large walled garden. The house itself is still haunted by the ghost of glories past. The slate long roof, the slender Georgian windows that sit so sweetly in the sandstone walls. Despite all this dilapidated grace, once in, you're in until you're out, if you get my meaning.

My fellow inmates are largely of the gentler sex, fifty in all including just eight men. There are also eight cottages in the grounds occupied by ancient, and not so ancient married couples. I see little of them, except when I spy into their golf buggy world when, they go scooting, strolling, or hobbling, round the grounds.

My earliest companion when I arrived was Geoff who's from another planet, he is brilliant, brilliant in a geeky way, but at least he's compos mentis, unlike some of the others who are all totally hopeless old farts, not gah-gah exactly, but more of them later. Geoff and I are allowed out but we have to sign the book and say where and when we're going. We wear green wrist bands with a little button. There are other coloured bands for various states of dilapidation. We sneak a pint or two about twice a week and Geoff likes his fish and chips and rather fancies the lady who makes the chips. I feel she rather gives her profession a bad name as she has to be fourteen stones, two hundred pounds or more.

The door closes and the pretty carer sings 'goodnight' and the cold loneliness sweeps over me. It never leaves me here because I know, that even my son and the grandkids in America, like to love me, but from a distance. I weep without tears, I find it hard to be alone despite the nice carers and the safe house where I now live, swallowed up and wrapped away like the useless old bastard that I've become.

I want sleep to come, so I can dream of my lovely wives, I loved them both. Now all gone, mourned for everyday and every night. How I loved them, how we laughed and planned and kissed, held hands and made love. How we brought things to those homes and how Johanna and me loved our son. How Margaret, my first, held me up when we lost all that money. How I held her as she died. It was black back then, my heart hurt with every beat, I wanted to die.

Of course, I did not die, and in less than two years I was in love again. At first, I felt I was betraying Margaret, but Johanna helped me feel alive again and even joined in my still saddened vigil of her predecessor. Johanna brought a selfless light that made me feel reborn and when our son David arrived it was a pinnacle of enormous joy.

Tonight, it's difficult to sleep because my leg hurts. My leg is the reason I'm in this 'home' for the hapless and hopeless. I was right as rain, living a robust life when I got pissed and fell down the stairs and broke my leg in two places. Shit, it hurt, I remember being so bloody cross as I lay hopelessly half way down the stairs – arse in the air and completely unable to move. I stayed there for eight hours till my cleaner came next morning. I must say I made a complete balls of things and it is true I was very unwell for quite a time. Anyway, David rushed from the States and made me promise I'd sell the house and move here. What a cock-up.

I wish I could go to sleep, this wretched leg really hurts. I'm not an alcoholic, I just like a drink now and again, but having nearly killed myself it's hard to persuade David that I can look after myself. It's my fucking fault. Please, please, can I go to sleep!

Morning comes early with first light, even the feather footed dawn wakes me up to face another day. Sometimes I feel I must make the best of it, other days I lay motionless, waiting for nothing. Nothing is a bugger, neither friend nor foe but I hate it nevertheless, nothing is a friend of loneliness, nothing makes me lazy, nothing makes me afraid. As I lay here dozing I can listen to it, bumping in my ears, things tinkle and creek, I'm not sure where. I hear the staff rattle the first tea cups of the day, the door open and close, and clatter of the dustmen.

Margaret and Johanna tussle for my dreamy awakening, and then I wake up to the cold reality. I stumble out of bed to face the day. The girls mumble as they melt into my morning, 'dress well there's a good boy' they say in chorus. 'Watch out for those stains now' says Johanna.

I stretch and feel my gammy leg, I see myself potbellied in the mirror, a haircut vaguely in the style of Julius Caesar. I'm still me, however my eyes are smaller than ever, supporting outrageous bags. Without my glasses I have a marked resemblance to Mr. McGoo. After a non-too athletic stretch, I sit in my bathroom contemplating the working of my much abused digestive system. The girls of my dreams have departed, they're not allowed in here. This is part of my morning ritual. One fall and they'll have some unfortunate carer to hold me up as I struggle into my underwear. Men's underwear, now there's a trial, y-fronts zed bends and all. Invented by a virgin who wanted to stay that way! Whoops! I'm being sexist.

After shaving and showering, and shouting to an enquiring carer as to my being alive and well, I dress carefully. My check shirt, my brogue shoes which get ever more difficult to get on, they are not a pair in the traditional sense. Since the accident of my army days I've had td to have a special shoe for my right foot. It takes an age to put on and take off, I have a special shoe horn. The shoe horn is one of my dearest possessions. If I lost it I don't know what I'd do. All this takes an age. Today, I select my smart tweedy but ancient jacket and silk handkerchief! A final check in the mirror and John Betts is ready for the day.

Today 'nothing' is not allowed. 'Cummon you old git, remember your Sergeant-major of all those years ago; Shoulders back, chin pointing down, neck in your collar and stand straight, bad leg or no. Right!' Off I go, hobbling on my walking stick down to start a new day. Pretending I have something to do.

Nothing follows me, my life I know is nearly over. Must I wait? What am I waiting for?

Chapter 2

Swallow Hall was once a very grand place, well outside the town and set in lush formal gardens within the estate wall. Now alas time has caught up with the rambling building, as it has the tumble-down town that has itself tumbled to new lows. Still, 'Swallow House' as it is now, is a home for the ancient and the hopeless, some well-heeled folk as well as those sponsored by the council. To stay here costs as much as you can afford, a small fortune for some, so that the complement is made up of the well-to-do and not so well-to-do.

I suppose I am one of the better off. The place is a curious mix of rich and poor, some old biddies who look close to the morgue, are bedecked with jewels that radiate the decadence of the wearers, others, the minority, wear the same clothes every day, sagging, fading like the wearers. The old crones stagger about on Zimmer frames or career around in electrically driven chairs, maintaining their strict social cliques like ducks on a small pond. The accents cut the air with a sharp English knife, everyone is 'frightfully' this or 'me dear' that. Some seem content to talk and to listen to gibberish. All part of the business of decay I suppose.

Swallow House has two floors around a sort of quadrangle, the ground floor houses the common rooms, excepting that portion where there are bedroom suites for the chronically infirm and those with dementia. Or 'the Lockup' as some call it. We seldom see these people, unless one keeps an eye out for the late or early visits of Morgan's Undertakers who slip in and out like large black beetles at irregular intervals. There are degrees of dementia, I mean some days I can't remember what day it is, or for that matter where I am. But the confusion I don't think lasts for long.

The out buildings are in much the same state as me, decrepit and crumbling, except of course for the pristine cottages for the married couples. I can't help but loathe them, they have something I do not, they have relative youth, wives and partners who love them, their own communal lounge and restaurant and even motor cars.

In these gently decaying gardens and amongst the sandstone eaves is where the swallows come to build their nests and swoop about the grounds. I suppose they've always come, to rest after their heroically long journeys from Africa. I gather that Swallow farm preceded Swallow Hall and House, so I suppose these little fellows have been coming and going for centuries. Their elegant acrobatics are almost too quick for my old eyes, but they cheer me up in the evenings and I have taken to coming into the garden to watch them before supper. They'll be darting about when I'm gone, - good for them.

It is morning and I sit on the patio, the sun rises over the trellis, the roses are not yet at their peak. A lady with huge breasts and extravagant cardigan sits a little way away and she seems to stare into space. She mutters to herself. Her hair is silver and despite her enormous bosom she looks frail, gaunt, as if all her weight has migrated to her chest. Should I talk to her? I did make a quiet salutation but she ignored me in her mumbling. I decide to make another effort – not to do nothing!

"Good morning." I speak loudly this time. "What a nice morning it is."

She continues to mumble. I huff. Then I notice she has a prayer book in her hand and I assume she's at her morning prayer. Alternatively of course might be that she's on the wrong end of the dementia scale. I huff some more, my dalliance with religion has long since passed, and I wander off to the morning room where the staff are just putting out the coffee.

"Good morning Mr. Butts" says the large but pretty carer who hails from Bulgaria or somewhere in the east of Europe.

12

"Betts,… but good morning." I reply, she looks confused.

I feel anxious, there are already groups of garrulous ladies gathering and making their way to breakfast. I am a stranger here despite my five months residence. The feeling of not belonging and being on my own amongst this insufferable crowd of spoiled rich and poor old farts is almost overwhelming. It is as if I'm in a glass box and everyone else is outside chattering inanities and twittering for the sake of the noise they make. The morning room is large with lovely wood panelled walls, pictures of various nobles hang unseen. The carpets are pink and thick, but worn in places, so that footsteps are seen and not heard. The only sound is the chirping of the ladies' morning chorus and the clink of imported china.

I hope Geoff comes down soon, he's company. We don't have much in common except we like cricket and rugby. Geoff is a bit of a duffer frankly, despite his academic achievements but he's kind and easy going, which is more than can be said of me.

Here comes Joan the General Manager, tall and attractive a fifty something, unmarried career woman, who is determinedly charming and at the same time authoritative.

"Good morning John," she smiles radiantly, her makeup perfect, her fragrance delicious. "And what are you up to today? There's the art class at eleven, you were very good at that when you had a go, they miss you, you know."

In her perfect way she is so fucking smug! I want to shout that I don't want to paint and watch all those pathetic old ladies daubing like chimps. But I don't,

"A bit messy for me Joan, but I'll think about it, I have a good book on the go just now."

Satisfied she's made an effort she glides smoothly on. I find I'm sniffing her perfume as she slips away, the aroma reminds me of Margaret.

Here comes Geoff, he's a lot younger than me, though I like to think that I'm livelier, that is except for my gammy leg. Geoff is tall and like most of us, what hair he has is silver white, he wears glasses which make him look myopic, although he can read a scoreboard at cricket better than me. He always wears a grin, it's part of his weaker mind perhaps. There,- I'm being unkind again. Geoff, always wears odd socks, he does this deliberately so he can start conversations which inevitably start, "Oh dear I seem to have odd socks on." He does this everywhere, at the races, the cricket, in the pub, it annoys me more than I can say, but he's the only close pal I've got so I go along with it and pretend what a surprise it is, even if it's the third time that particular day.

We sit in the same place we always do and we spend a huge amount of our time avoiding those inmates we can't bear. This is quite a long list starting with two other men. One is a miserable man who complains about his health all day and the other a retired Bishop whose family is very well-to-do. The ex-Bishop was only a minor or auxiliary bishop but he carries a prayer book with him always and is a pompous self-appointed chaplain. He is, in my not too humble opinion a boring wind-bag who has never seen life to any extent except the country parishes which his family underwrote. He insists on being called 'Bishop Steven' which annoys me further. I annoy him by calling him Mister Boyd, which as far as I am concerned is his proper name. .

The other gent is Dan, I can't recall his full name, he complains nonstop about being eighty or whatever age he is. He speaks as if every breath is his last, a sort of pathetic whisper. He is clearly close to the dementia lockup and often asks me about rugby games of forty or fifty years ago.

"Did you see Dickie Jeeps? What a win on Saturday, was it in Cardiff?" He whispers, smiling, and then in a trice asks "pass the sugar will you Harry."

I can't help but shout at him hoping he'll speak up but he never does. And who the hell is Harry? Who cares? Without being unkind I think he's longing to 'kick the bucket' and that each day is a tremendous trial for him. His pallor is like parchment and he is very bent so that he's always looking at the floor. Boring old bugger, except these dashes into the past, all of which, seem completely random. He takes us all by surprise, boring then startling, and that's a fact.

Much to my chagrin the Bishop and Dan both sit at our table. I mumble good morning.   Dan takes an age to settle into his dining chair. We all wait, then The Bishop says grace, whilst I noisily rattle my cereal bowl and tea cup.

"No need for all this Mr. Boyd." I say it quietly, and the Bishop chooses not to hear me.

Dan shuffles interminably and shakes his breakfast dishes with such a tremor that he sounds like a misplaced and out of tune percussionist.

Geoff is much nicer than me, he bows his head during grace, and helps Dan to pour the weak tea which is our breakfast lot each day. He and Boyd have a conversation about the weather and the cricket, though in my view Boyd knows bugger all about the game.

Geoff and me are due to have a day out, starting at around ten, we've booked a taxi to Taunton to watch Somerset play Gloucestershire, anything to get out of this place with its constant hen house babble. The other men are all around the eighty mark, Peter is an ex-soldier and a very decent sort. The others I hardly know and they always stick together so we are, as it were, two groups, two cliques with poor Dan, wavering between the groups and life and death, and he clings to anyone who will talk to him other than the dreaded Boyd.

Let me say that of the ladies there one or two who would come under the description of attractive. I have not yet felt able to make any advances as I feel I would be being unfaithful to my departed wives Margaret and Johanna. Nevertheless there is a sneaking and inescapable desire to make contact with these targets of delight. I am at odds with myself. I am, I know, cutting off my nose to spite my face. I am not the man I was. I have no confidence, I am afraid of what impression I make, I am afraid of what my deceased wives will think, I am afraid. I find it impossible to cross the line, maybe I'm afraid of rejection, or the defences of the gaggles of women whose closed ranks look formidable.

That is not to say that I have not been approached by several of the ladies. However, I have to say that the attention that I received was not from the quarters I might think desirable. Or am I making all these excuses up. I have reverted to my shy childhood, I am afraid. Indeed, my response I fancy, may well have created an impression that I am distant and cold. I am not. I am lonely and I grieve and it is very hard.

I spend an unreal amount of time dreaming of my past, I remember the fire..........*A small boy's winter in 1937*

I remember the fire, burning brightly in the grate, I tugged on my wellies with excited haste, as I watched through the window the snowflakes fall, huge and white, softly deadening the din and brightening the light. Mother's there, she's casting spells on mouth-watering tastes and delicious smells.

I'm outside, the snow whiter than I ever saw, my fingers cold, numb, the burning frosts gnaw. Snowballs whiz by, snowmen take shape, and the cold and wetness make me shake. The snow melts icily into my socks, and makes icicles in my blonde and curly locks. I don't want to go home; but the cold dictates. Reluctant, shivering I retreat in haste.

Mum rubs me down, at first she's scolding, and then I'm warmed, with her arms round me folding. Then big sister's home, she's bravely boasting she stayed outside while I was in,- toasting, Soon all scrubbed and warm, we sit down together. The pie gives up its glories, all in good measure. The magic outside once more starts to entice, full tummies help us forget the bitter cold ice.

Dad's come home early, back from his toil. He smells of work and tobacco and oil, his smile supports his fine grey moustache. And despite the weather he's inclined to laugh, his day's been without the fun we enjoyed, his lorry's in snow, quite unemployed.

All filled with the comfort of the steaming hot food. Dad, decides to stop work and stay home with the brood. So he gently ignores our mother's cry, and helps with socks and boots not

quite dry, so that we kids can build and make it
our own, the biggest snowman in the whole of
the town. Dad and two kids from Mum's
scolding embrace into the enchanted garden
they race, where the deep white snow lies so
blindingly clean and frames the black coal shed
in its brilliant gleam.

How different this palace of decrepitude is, still
seventy seven years is a long time ago.

At eighty four, I have few things to look forward
to. Going to the cricket today is perhaps one of
them, although I am ambivalent about the effort
versus the reward. Geoff is an amiable
companion and I know I'm lucky to have him as
a friend. Although I think he's a bit on the slow
side his background belies this. He was indeed a
Professor of Physics if you please, I discovered
this quite by accident when I noticed all these
journals piled high in his rooms. All completely
incomprehensible to me about particle physics –
whatever that is. Then, when a visitor came, a

22

bright faced chap about thirty, he greeted Geoff with great deference and addressed him as Professor Watkins, you could have knocked me over with a feather. I think perhaps my knowledge of the subject limits his desire to say anything with enthusiasm. Geoff has been a lifelong bachelor, and he has never mentioned his family except a few mumbles about his father who, I gather, was also an academic.

Since I discovered that Geoff was a very distinguished scientist, that discovery has done little to bring us closer together. I just wish he'd lighten up a bit.

We men have rooms adjacent to each other, the suites are all the same, lounge TV etc,, small kitchen area, nice big bedroom with bathroom en-suite. We are allowed some personal effects, I have lots of pictures, grainy ones of my Dad before he went off to the war, me looking smart with my platoon, Margaret and the wedding group, I looked so nervous. There are pictures too of Johanna and David at his christening, his wedding. The pictures then stop, the happy tale of John Betts, no more Johanna, an empty wall.

I have my writing desk, where I sometimes lock away contraband scotch amongst my poetry books. I am addicted to the poets of the Great War.

I also have a music centre, that's not what David called it. I am encouraged to listen to my music through ear phones so not to disturb the other guests. I suspect they are mostly deafer than me, so who cares?

I spend much of my life dodging the dreaded Boyd, and to a lesser extent the cripple Dan as he staggers about staring at his feet. He seems always to be calculating when the next disaster is to befall him. Dan has a family, their name is legion, and they are many, as it says in the good book. They visit frequently creating a disturbance as fourth generation offspring fawn and make an unnecessary din. I have a feeling they are gathering like vultures before the feast, another unqualified and malevolent thought.

The regulations here are quite strict, alcohol is rationed and every time I want to go out, I have to sign a book of what time I leave, where I am going and what time I expect to be back. It's just like my boarding school in my distant youth. Yes, I went away to school which was brutal. My dad wasn't rich by any means and I only got into that hell hole because I won a scholarship for folk who otherwise could not afford the fees.

I still remember the heart break of home sickness, the anger and the beatings, the useless teachers and the freezing dormitories. I hated the place, the only thing that could be said for it was that when I joined the army it made it all seem very easy. I would have stayed in the army if I hadn't broken my ankle very badly, so I was released as a young subaltern with a limp and not much idea of what I wanted to do. Sixty odd years has passed since those heady days. I feel almost that I have come whole circle.

Once a week Ms. McCann, Joan, the sexy manager 'pops in' as she puts it, for a chat. I know what she's up to, she's reporting to my son on my health, temper and behaviour. She smiles and shimmies about pretending to be looking after my welfare, but I know she's checking up on the drinks cabinet, my medicine cabinet and any other bloody part of my existence that she can prod and pull around. She's like that ghastly matron at school. Except of course she's much better looking.

Other monthly meetings include my solicitor, who helps with my son's arrangements about power of attorney, they send some whipper-snapper, the boss, is getting on himself.

The Doctor or nurse comes at least once a month, and I have to be on parade for check-ups. Bloody waste of time I think. I know when I'm not up to speed I don't need these busy bodies to tell me. All goes on the Bill of course, none of this free NHS here, at least not for the paying residents.

Chapter 3

It's a nice day, the sun is shining. Our taxi driver is a cheery chap who regularly picks us up for our Thursday jaunts. We've signed out until dinner time, so I'm looking forward to some good cricket and some aimless chat with the other pensioners in our enclosure.

"Good morning, professor, good morning Mr Betts." Our Taxi man is not from these parts.

"Good morning, Mohamed." Smiles back Geoff.

"What oh!" say I as I can never remember his name. The taxi is an ancient Mercedes and Geoff and I settle comfortably into the creased leather seats.

At the cricket ground all we ancients are corralled into an area near the pavilion, marked 'Senior Citizens' so we don't have too much time travelling to the bars and the conveniences. The latter is pretty damned important for a group whose average age is late seventies. I am

regarded as a senior amongst the seniors –
bloody old!

I can never remember any of the names of my
fellow oldies, neither can anyone else, so we all
call each other 'old chap'.

It's all "Good morning, dear boy, or my friend,
or old fella'".

Geoff breaks the convention some times by
settling down on our bench and telling me that I
remember Simon when I clearly do not. The
same goes for Bryn, Jonathan, John and all the
rest of them. They are an anonymous group of
pleasant but bland, gentlemen all. Let me not
exaggerate we are not a crowd of thousands, we
are about twenty on a good day and today
despite the weather about fifteen.

I shuffle along the bench over the peeling paint,
now peeling and greying like the skin on my
withered arms. I'm warm, should have put on a
lighter jacket. Strange but I sometimes feel the

heat and sometimes not. I always feel the cold though, and tend to overcompensate with heavy clothes which today is obviously wrong.

Geoff in his patient way chats about Somerset cricket, after he's drawn attention to his odd socks. He seems to be able to reel off a whole load of statistics. He talks too of the personalities, who's batting and in which order and the like. Good for him, it occurs to me that I have very little grasp of this detail despite my delight in watching the game unfold. I try to avoid talking about 'when I was at school or with the regiment when I was this batsman or that.'

"I remember scoring 86 off some pretty serious speed when I was in the forces, on a quick wicket too……"

Who cares? I certainly don't.

 That's what everyone else does and I find it hard to join in with this delusional self-aggrandisement. Despite this, I am content, listening to my fellow old farts waffling about their pathetic pasts.

In the morning sun, I bask under my old panama and my dark glasses and remember…….

It is 1940, I am ten years old, we are playing cricket in the little park behind my house. Its summer holidays, and I'm still unsure of my cricketing skills. Colin Evans who's about the same size as me, is so good he knocks the ball miles no matter who is bowling.

"C'ummon, six and you're out!" Shouts Mal Morgan, he's tall and gangly with a shock of hair that almost stands straight up. He has a darker complexion than the rest of us. He lives over near the railway station, where a lot of tough boys live. Tougher than me, and they have a gang. My dad says they're not good boys and I should be careful who I play with.

We all go to the church primary school, most of us have just done our exam for the grammar school. Of the cricketing gang I know only two of us will pass the exam. That's what we all expect, I live near the park, they live near the station, my dad owns my house and they live in council houses. That's how it is.

At the back of the park is a pond, and beyond the pond is the steel works. Steam rises giving the pond an air of mystery, in fact it's a cooling pond for the steel mills. Despite prohibition notices we play there often. There are swans and ducks and a little island shrouded in bushes and surrounded by reeds standing like soldiers guarding the island mysteries.

There are real soldiers, my dad says there's going to be a war. I'm not at all clear what that means. Will it be like in the pictures? Mum says she hopes there won't be a war. I think it might be fun.

"What's this mum?"

I'm holding a floppy white balloon half filled with liquid."

My mother shrieks, "Uugh throw it away, now!..in the bin."

I wondered why, but then, used contraceptives weren't in my domain.

My house is in a terrace, I live there with my mum and dad and my sister who is older than me. She goes to the girls' grammar school. Jennifer is much admired by some of the boys. I don't know why, she's very bossy……

"Come on John, time for a beer and a sandwich." Geoff squeezes past me and we troop into the bar for my customary pint and sandwich.

"89 for one, not bad before lunch" it's that bloke who never buys a round, making himself a part of the small group that includes Geoff, me and whatshisname.

"What would you like?" Geoff as always falls for the creeps and hangers on.

"A pint of Tribute." Is the prompt reply, "thanks!" an afterthought.

I didn't used to listen very much but now I do. It's as if I'm too tired to lead a conversation any more. I can remember little of this morning's cricket but I do remember me playing in People's Park in 1940. Still the beer tastes nice so does the sandwich.

The lunch break is forty minutes and the times goes by quickly punctuated by members of the group using the comfort room.

"Are you all right?" It's Geoff again being solicitous.

"Of course I'm all right, bugger off Geoff, I'm fine, thinking about another pint, what do you think?"

"I'd leave it, if I were you." Geoff retorts, in a neutral sort of way.

"Then we'll have one, Ok?"

"Ok." and I order two more pints being careful to avoid the freeloader.

The day passes, two hours then tea, two hours to end of play, then the taxi ride back to Swallow House. This is as good as it gets.

Of course we have to stop for fish and chips. For Geoff this is the highlight of his week. I watch as he transmogrifies into an aged Errol Flynn, he makes really bad jokes about cod and haddock, and praises the modest shop for excellence of its fare. I have to sit whilst this pathetic Lothario treads his stuff. I wonder idly what would happen if two tonne 'Tessie' responded to him. Don't think Geoff is much of a sprinter actually. I suspect that Geoff loved his particle physics more than anything or anybody hence his late fascination with two tonne Tessie and what could have been. Nonetheless I enjoy the grub, as does our Taxi driver whose name is Salman. Salman always does our return journey, he seems to have an instinct about when we are to stop for fish and chips. Mohamed, obviously works mornings only, or perhaps Salman keeps the evening fish and chips trip to himself. Geoff tips him as well, the silly bugger.

In my room, I take off my heavy sports jacket and help myself to a scotch and water. I sit to watch the late news but then…

The war is all round us, the interview was in a grand office, I don't recall where. My mum takes me and explains that I'm perhaps going away to school to Finsbury College where my rich cousin Michael went. I am shown into an office and a fat clergyman who is, I learn, the headmaster of Finsbury College. I am not nervous, I am curious, what was all this about?

The questions come and I remember the Head Master asking me, "If I saw a railway train and it sounded its whistle, what would happen first? I would see the steam or hear the whistle? Any ten year old would know that answer and I was no exception. The fat clergyman, I'll swear, looked impressed. I couldn't wait to go home and out to play.

Mal Morgan and his gang gathered by the canal and often walked under the long tunnel, fetid, stinking and refuse laden. Rats occasionally scampered as the gang clattered through, throwing stones, fooling and wrestling each other to the brink of disaster. No one I can remember fell in, though on many a time I shrieked in fear, much to the mirth of Mal and his close gangsters. I can smell the yellowed sluggish canal, see the rubbish half submerged and still stiffen at the echoing squeal of the scampering rodents.

They never really let me in. I lived the wrong side of the park you see. I was about to separate, forever, away to Finsbury College with all the rich kids.

There's a knock on the door. I wake from my reverie.

"Come in" and in breezes one of the male supervisors whose name 'Alex' is pinned to his uniform.

"Evening Mr Betts, how are you this evening. I've brought your pills, and checking if you need anything? Need any help at all?"

"No thank you, put the pills over there, there's a good fellow, then, I'll hit the sack, thanks…"

"I'll just get a glass of water, Mr Betts," which he does and the proffers the glass and my four tablets, one pink, one brown, two white and of various sizes, he waits over me till I obediently take my evening medicines. I hate this bloody standing over me, as if I am some sort of halfwit. They do it every night. I do as I'm told. I don't turn round, and wish Alex a curt good night without bothering to look back.

My room is warm and the bed comfortable, but it is the loneliest place on earth. Sleep never comes easily though I desperately wish that it will. Because when I sleep I live again and hear my girls laugh, I see them plainly together, despite their differences they are the same, age, place and time. I listen to them chat, they talk about me.

"He was a silly boy when I met him first, he limped like an injured lamb."

"He was angry that you'd gone when he met me, he was like a wasp not knowing where to sting."

"You made him happy."

"You made him happy"

And they laugh, and then first light comes, and I wake.

Chapter 4

Another day, I wake in my 'Home' suite of rooms. The accommodation is fine, my bedroom is calm, the bed comfy, the wardrobes copious, the carpet thick and soft under my feet, its all lovely there's no doubt about that. Despite the bells and whistles, the quiet comfort, the privacy, it is empty, there is no soul, the house has central heating but not the warmth of home and never will be my real home. I've been here some twenty weeks and it seems much longer than that.

After my catastrophic fall, I was manacled to various beds in the health services both public and private. I suppose hospitals are never nice places for the inmates, and it certainly wasn't great for me. My injuries were very painful and I foolishly did my forward roll down the stairs on a weekend when the hospital emergency services are at a low ebb. In any event, it was all very uncomfortable, very painful and to make matters worse I broke the leg with the gammy ankle. This posed the medics problems, which resulted in a complete cock up and they had to break my leg again because of some spurious reason, though I reckon the weekend crew had no idea what they were doing with an eighty something drunk who'd been doing acrobatics.

Be that as it may, my son David travelled across the 'pond' almost on a weekly basis and did his absolute best, I know. But, really he wanted me locked up safely somewhere, anywhere. I hated myself for making him travel so much and work so hard, I almost hated him for insisting I move here. I was in no position to fight him although I wanted, and still want, to go home.

Home is where the heart is, and it's not here. Swallow House will never be my home. It's an amalgam of my old school, a hotel and a geriatric nursing home, but it is not and never will be home.

I came from Apple Tree House in Bingham, twenty odd miles away, that is where my heart is, any way what's left of my heart. That is where I nursed my lovely Johanna when she was pregnant, that is where David grew up. That is where I lived and loved living, where the creaking cellar door spoke of good things to come, where the draughty kitchen window reminded me of how cosy we were on winter nights. Where the pictures of Margaret were dusted and cared for by Johanna, where exam results were opened, where David brought his bride to be, where I slept in the downy warmth of home. I miss all that terribly, I miss the blossom of the trees, my neighbours and the milkman. I weep sometimes because I am no longer home, and no one, not even David understands. Nobody understands.

It's not as if I haven't been around. I've had a good life. My early days perhaps were amongst the hardest. In 1940 my Dad was called up. I was already in that dreadful school where the war was an excuse for maltreatment of often displaced children. I missed my mum and dad and my sister, everything was ghastly, the food, the clothes, the beds even the teachers, who were all ancient as all the young men went off to war. The whole regime was cruel and unforgiving, it was 'Tom Brown's Schooldays.' In spades. The prefects were all bastards, and beat the juniors on a whim. In my case that seemed every day.

I couldn't get home even for half term, and my mum who was then working as a secretary in some factory, could never get time to come and see me. And then in 1943 my dad was killed. He was killed, I didn't know where. I only knew he was dead. There was just a telegram to mum. It was in the Easter holiday. No funeral, no letters from the King, nothing! Dad was not going to be home again. It was as if the family were slammed shut, no longer in the mainstream, no longer a family, just Mrs Betts and her kids. I went back to school for one more term where no one took a single moment to talk about my dad, no one put their arm around me as I cried in chapel, and then it all ended.

 Mum brought me home and I loved her for it. We became a family again. At fourteen, I was her man. It was my first realisation of grief, as my mother wept quietly in her lonely bed, we wept as well, Jennifer and me bravely, separately in an unspoken sharing of grief.

Then followed the days of growing into manhood, discovering myself, times of confusion, and times of revelation. Girls, getting to know them and not being sure why or how to behave. The first marvellous fumbles, the thrills of cuddles and kisses. The first heat of hearts beating so close, so close as to be unreal.

Jennifer my sister was very pretty, and had hordes of admirers. I was jealous in a fraternal way and more than once crassly interrupted her careful admission of new boyfriends. Despite that, Jenni as I used to call her, and I always got on well, she had a great sense of mischief and laughter which she sustained all her lovely life.

The war ended and I was called up into the Army, I decided to serve three years on a short service commission and I thoroughly enjoyed it.

Did you shave this morning....Sir"

"Yes Sergeant Major,"

"And was the bathroom crowded .... Sir"

"As usual, Sergeant Major."

The Sergeant Major took a step back. He nodded in his strange tick of a way, his Welsh Guards peek almost touching the bridge of his nose.

"Well, you must have shaved the man standing next to you Sah!! You're a disgrace .. and well.... Sir turning out like a tramp! Turning out like a sack of spuds ... Sah! Is that the reason I call you Sir is it?"

"No Sergeant Major."

*"Mr. Betts speak when I ask you if you please...
Sir. The reason I call you Sir is Sir, because you
are supposed to be a leader of men. Not a
tramp, not a sack of spuds and definitely not an
Officer Cadet who can't shave properly." The
volume of the Sergeant Majors voice had started
as a whisper, I almost leaned in to listen, but by
the time the Sergeant Major got to the 'shave
properly' bit he almost deafened the square.*

*John Betts or Officer Cadet Betts of the
Gloucestershire Regiment almost shook in his
sparkling boots. Sgt Major Morgan could
frighten an elephant.*

*Some twelve weeks later, Sgt Major Morgan
shook me, Second Lieutenant Betts by the hand.*

*"Good luck Sir, You'll do your regiment proud
Sir."*

*He snapped to attention and I wanted to hug
this giant of a man who had fathered the platoon
from a shambolic and random assembly of*

young men into at least for the most part, a cadre of well-trained infantry officers.

My mother stood by, unsure about her son's choice of the army instead of just two years' service like all the other boys.

My relationship with my mum seemed to have been segmented into pre-boarding school and post boarding school and the mighty bond we'd formed after dad was killed. The changes were immense for us both, I understood even at fourteen that I had to grow up, and grow up I did. There was no dad, no more being lifted and thrown in the park, no more ball games, no more watching rugby together.

Then without any warning, my new dad arrived three years after my real dad had died. I remember my mum introducing Walter, I could tell how nervous she was. Jenni and I both reacted differently. I was polite but distant, I tried desperately to pretend that things were as they used to be, but of course they weren't. I

47

felt miserable when I went to bed, I knew things were not as before. Since then of course I'd worked it out, Mum had kissed and cuddled and shagged Walter and as nice as he tried to be, I found there was part of me that hated him.

Jenni was confused too. She always loved her mother and her father but in different ways. Mother had kept the family together and Dad had just gone off and died. Dad had died an unsung hero, he had left a huge hole in her heart. Who was this Walter she confided in me, what did mum see in him?

On Aldershot camp square I plotted a course of my own. I would not go to university for sure, I didn't know what if anything I would study, may be I'd make a career in the army.

"Thank you for everything Sgt Major." My eyes misted over.

A smart salute, a snapped about turn and the Sergeant Major marched sharply away, I was on my own.

As Second Lieutenant Betts I joined my regiment in Germany part of the British Army of the Rhine (BAOR), it was like going back to school. I found my fellow junior officers all of similar background and one in four were like me short service commissioned to guarantee not being confined to the ranks for the duration of national service. I was amongst the huge numbers to be 'called up'.

Like school, the strict hierarchy ruled with an astonishing rigidity.

 My first month was an agony of doing all the jobs no one else wanted. I was orderly Officer for my first four weekends in charge of an empty barracks commanding a group of soldiers most of who didn't want to be there any more than 'Mr Betts' as I was universally addressed.

My first Officer pal was Ben Trimmer, though six months my senior he enjoyed rugby as I had in my school days. I soon made a place for myself in the regimental team where I lived and loved a completely different side of army life. Captain Cox the team skipper was very much the leader and he was also the main man as far as the team was concerned. All the men called him 'Sir' or 'Coxy' but there remained a respect and comradeship which I had never seen before. .

I became altogether more comfortable, I was a member of the Regiment, a strange family of brothers, from junior subaltern to Colonel.

It was with three of my brother junior officers that I went out on the town. It was just about my first free weekend. The drinking started early with Trimmer leading the way.

"Cummon men, down to the Prussian Club. Time for Betts to see the world."

By nine o' clock all four of us were much the worse for wear we sat at a table laden with beer and eight places, I was already so drunk I barely noticed the arrangements when the four girls arrived.

Of the delectable ladies who joined us, next to me sat the formidable Magda.

"You are Johnny, a new boy, yes?"

She smelt divine, her perfume overwhelming, her make-up like nothing I'd ever seen before. Confusion rained down on my 19 year old virgin frame. I cannot quite remember what I said. Something like.. "How do you do."

They shrieked with laughter.

I was until that time certainly a virgin and it was with the accommodating Magda, a pneumatic blond some eight years my senior, that I consummated my lust and became a man. However much I enjoyed the experience it was somewhat vaguer than it might have been, addled as I was by a surfeit of alcohol and severe lack of skill. However the alcohol slowed the rising of the sap so that Magda with consummate skill 'blooded' another young British officer, a task she found both pleasurable and rewarding. Lieutenant Trimmer settled the bill with decorum and I was carried back to barracks unaware that my great adventure had been all part of the regimental family plan.

Two weeks later the Rugby team gathered for a home game.   It all ended badly for me with a horrendous injury to my ankle, an injury that turned out to be a disaster. The disaster had been compounded by less than competent first aid on that fateful weekend in Osnabruck

The consequence was that I was kept in hospital, my plaster cast removed and the following Monday I underwent surgery to correct a complex fracture of ankle and lower leg system, not one bone but several bones and ligaments had been damaged.

Two weeks later I underwent further surgery and it became apparent that my injuries were limb threatening and that arrangements were made for me to be returned to the RAMC HQ Hospital at Aldershot.

In Aldershot things did not improve and my only consolation was a young nurse called Anna who made me much more relaxed during her night shifts. Whilst my future as an athlete faded my sexual life skills were considerably enhanced. Nevertheless I missed the life, I missed my regimental brothers, I had been borne again and now it was all coming to a shambolic end.

In the meantime Walter married mum and she became Mrs. Ramsey, even less a member of my family, I was still very ambivalent about Walter, I knew that mum loved him but my boyish cuckoo syndrome still lurked deep within me. Walter, it turned out, was a wonderful guy who loved my mum with an obvious passion. He was always kind and considerate and inclusive with both Jennifer and me. It still took me years to really allow myself to care for him as I know my mum desperately wanted. I hope she forgave me.

In hospital boredom was a huge problem as the days dragged by. X-rays and pain killers were the order of the day.

"Silly fucking game – rugby, I see more of you buggers than training casualties. When will you guys ever learn?" The chief medic was not impressed.

It was the Chaplin who delivered the news that I was to be discharged from my army commission due to my injuries. I was expecting it but when the news came I was devastated, although of course the prospect had certainly crossed my mind. Despite that, I felt surprisingly hurt, I felt grief envelope me. I was losing my family for the second time.

I just nodded and held back the tears.

That night Anna visited, she sat beside me on my bed. I declined her ministrations and we sat together, me dosing and inhaling Anna's strange mixture of perfume and hospital detergent. I drifted off to sleep what a lovely girl Anna was.

And now this, I was to be cast away from the regiment, my new family who I had in such a short time grown to love.

Col Winter arrived an hour late on his rounds.

"Well young man how are you doing? Look I'm very sorry but I can't see another way, I've had to recommend your discharge I don't think that ankle of yours is going to be up to snuff for at least a year and maybe more. Certainly won't be playing that bloody silly game anyway for a while yet."

The Colonel looked ill at ease, "I'm really sorry old chap, I hate good guys like you having to quit, it almost indicates that we're less than competent. In your case the damage was so great I don't think we could have done any better and there's more surgery to come, I hope we'll get you out of here on you two pins. But it will take a while yet."

"What's the long term view Colonel?" I was desperately sad, what I'd heard so far sounded awful.

"We'll not send you to the civilian hospital until you're clearly on the mend, what I mean by that is the Army will look after you with every tool at our disposal. As far as your injury is concerned I think you have a chance of a fairly full recovery, but I don't think any of that rugby stuff will be on the cards."

I still didn't really understand what the colonel was driving at. "Will I be able to walk and run?"

"Walk certainly, maybe with some support for a while, but I don't think you'll be running for a good while yet. I think you have to take one step

at a time if you see my meaning – sorry for the pun- but each patient is different." The colonel shuffled his files and produced the latest x-ray. "the ankle is probably the most complex joint we have, it certainly has the most complex moving set of parts both bone and tissue. In your case the first aid was strictly speaking correct but there were complications that were impossible to see. We've corrected most of the bone damage and one more surgery I think may make a huge difference, but the ligament damage may take a very long time to heal, that may also need further surgery. All may go swimmingly but it will be long and complex road. You are young and fit so I have every confidence that the prognosis will be good. Up to you though, as much as up to us. Physiotherapy will be vital in your recovery and the Army is pretty good at that. I hope we can start that in a week or so."

There was a silence, The Chaplin appeared as if by magic, he the first to speak. "You have the strength John, here.." he tapped above his heart,

"You will recover and find a new life where you will be an inspiration to others, I'm sure of it."

The Medic departed in a flurry of his surgical greens, squeaking down the polished corridor in his theatre boots.

As he took his leave Coxy arrived disturbing the balance of my bed with his huge weight. The Chaplin made his excuses and left.

"The Colonel sends his best, we were all very sad to hear of the discharge decision ... very bad luck, very bad luck."

"Roll of the dice Sir, I'm pissed off but the card's been dealt and I have no other choice than to play what I am given. What brings you to Aldershot? Very kind to come all this way to see me."

Coxy laughed, "You know how generous the MOD is, no I'm glad to have the chance to see you but I'm on a course at Staff College, hopefully on my way to field rank... you know the

Army, we all do as we're told. What about you, what are you going to do?"

"I was just talking to the padre about that I have no bloody idea, university I guess but what after that, I have no idea at all."

Coxy unloaded a small pile of cards, from each Mess. A bottle of Scotch and a small package that he placed on the bed. I opened the cards, they came from my brothers in the officers' mess, one from the colonel and his lady, one from my platoon Sergeant, one from HQ Company and one from the Battalion rugby team. I felt moved to tears, when would I ever be part of something like this ever again? Coxy ruffled my hair, "Don't let them get you down John, one door closes but I'm sure another will open. Be good and get that ankle sorted - and that's an order."

I lay back and tried to sleep. I couldn't, so I idly unpacked the parcel that Coxy had left. It was a little silver rugby ball set on the regimental

Crest, It was engraved, To John Betts from his brother Officers – 'To your future'.

I closed my eyes and let the tears fall, I stared at the little silver trophy, all I had left from my army career of seven wonderful months.

I was discharged from Hospital/rehab and the army after ten month's service. Armed with a travel warrant a small amount of cash and a pronounced limp, I arrived at the new family home. Mum wrapped me in her arms, I could feel the slight reserve in her embrace as Walter looked on. Mum looked petite and attractive, the maturing country wife. My step father Walter, despite my inner denial, looked 'right' in this new rather splendid house. Walter was well to do, for the first time I had an inkling of how lucky mum had been to find a guy who was not only gentle and kind but also well off.

The warmth of mum's embrace revived the memory of our interdependence of five years before. That special mother son relationship, a bond with just the one unbroken link.

I held mum at arm's length, "It's good to be home Mum, you look well."

She gently stroked my face, "My soldier boy, I'm so sorry things didn't go to plan."

Chapter 5

It's a bloody miserable day, pissing down, summers were never like this when I was younger. The thing is, at eighty four, you dare not go out in the rain unless you want to risk some fatal influenza type ailment. Sometimes I think that an early end to this misery would be a good thing. Where will tomorrow lead anyway? I have no idea, no goals, no prospects. Shit and darkness ahead, that's growing old. This is when Swallow House is at its worst. These dreadful inmates are the only alternative to staying in my rooms. I could of course go to painting lessons with those half-witted old biddies, God forbid! I stamp about, debating whether to knock on Geoff's door but I have a feeling he'll be pouring over his particle physics journals.

I had a letter from David, they are all well and he will come and see me next week when he comes to London on business. I want to see him of course but I know the trip down here will be a hassle for him. Again I think it would be better if I were dead, and then he can get on with his life without worrying about me all the time. I never used to think like this till I fell down the bloody stairs. I cannot escape the fact that I am an old idiot who really brings little to the world. It is hard to remember that I am one of the lucky ones. I'm reasonably well off and warm and looked after, I have my hearing, my sight and I'm in pretty good shape despite my arthritis and of course my shitty leg. My memory plays tricks but it's still pretty good. At least, I think so.

University was a complete failure for me, all the other students had come straight from school, I was strangely advanced from my fellow students, ten months in the army had made such a difference. I suffered from acute sexual deprivation, after the ministrations of Nurse Anna I just couldn't think of anything else. Sex, was my obsession. My studies came a distant second, in lectures I scanned the halls for attractive girls in the hope that I could create a carnal liaison. I succeeded more than once, but those affairs were, as far as I remember, rather unsatisfactory because the young women fell so far short of Nurse Anna and her undoubted skills. At the end of my first year I was advised either to leave the College or possibly take another subject, following a catastrophic failure in my first year exams.

I am confused now, but thinking back I was confused then too. I was becoming a serial failure, first the army, now University. I felt ashamed of myself and felt I'd let Mum and Walter down.

"Mum, I think I'm going to get a job." The summer winds blew the apple blossoms gently against the conservatory windows. The kitchen was Mum's palace, spick and span. Stone flags on the floor, the cast iron stove, the brand new washing machine with its twin tubs. It was as modern as any kitchen in 1952.

"Don't be silly you have to go back to college and get your degree."

I clutched the letter of dismissal in my pocket, I had been waiting three weeks to break the news – I'd had the boot.

"Mum I'm not going back,…I failed my first years exams, it's over…sorry."

To be fair to Mum, she didn't weep and wail as I expected, she just stopped peeling the potatoes, shrugged. In that shrug, I can see now, the disappointment, the sorrow and the love. In that almost unnoticeable twitch of her delicate frame, my Mum swallowed her disappointment, reached down and made the decision to support this useless boy that was me. There was a moment of quiet and then she said,

"What are you going to do?"

"I've applied to Kitchco for a job as a salesman."

"A salesman! I don't think Walter will like that, let's see if he can get you a job in his business. I'm sure he'll find you something, he wants you there I know."

"Mum, I'm not going to work for or with Walter, ….I think he's a great guy, but I must make it on my own, no handouts, he's already made you happy and both Jen and I think he's worth his weight in gold, and he's done so much for us, I'm sorry Mum but I have to make a go of it on my own."

I hated the idea of becoming a salesman for plastic kitchen appliances, but there was something in me that wouldn't fall back on dear old Walter. There followed several heated debates about my future, but I limped off to my interview with Louis Mills a rather jolly fellow, who thought that plastics were the future of the world. Mills also got it into his head that I was some sort of war hero. To my everlasting shame I did nothing to put him right. And so it was I acquired my second hand Ford 8 and for the next year careered around the West Country and Wales flogging plastic kitchen ware.

The Ford 8 was splendidly reliable, it cost sixty pounds and did not have a heater. I got a pal of mine to rig up a fan heater which plugged into the innards of the dashboard. I used to call the car 'black beauty' and I talked to 'her' all the time, urging her up the hills and down the valleys of Wales and Dartmoor.

It was 1952, the great exhibition was over, my sales of plastic bowls, whisks spoons et al had exceeded Kitchco's expectations, and I was invited to take up a senior post in London where, I was informed, I could double my commission income, practically overnight.

In the meantime Walter had bought me a bicycle, a sporty type with drop handlebars. It was a great and thoughtful gift because pushing pedals was about the only thing I could do with my gammy leg. The bike was my keep fit option for the next thirty years. God bless Walter.

Much to Kitchco's disappointment I joined a company in Bristol, again in sales but this time in construction and engineering and I acquired a tiny flat just opposite the Cathedral Green. My new company car was bright and smart, I thought it was the bee's knees. I still went regularly to the hospital and it was there that I met Margaret Davies. It wasn't love at first sight or anything like that, true she was attractive, but I was unsure of myself, new job, new flat, new town. I thought nothing more about the pretty physiotherapist.

After my third physio session, there she was again, petit, efficient, and neat. She had dark hair, lovely green grey eyes. She remarked on how much stronger my leg had become.

"It's my bike, I cycle a lot now and that keeps my leg working."

"Good boy," she smiled down on me as she massaged the area at the bottom of my calf. "What else do you do then?"

"What do mean, what else do I do?"

She smiled again, an impish grin that transformed her face into a round radiant sun. It was then that I was dazzled.

I summed up the courage and invited her to supper in a rather posh place in Clifton. It was an old fashioned date and the beginning of my growing up as far as the opposite sex was concerned. And so our great romance grew, I fell in love, never to fall out of it whilst my lovely Margaret walked the earth.

We married in the spring of 1954, and bought our first house for one thousand two hundred and fifty pounds. Margaret's mum and dad and Walter supported us through those years when a Television was a luxury and fridge/freezers an American dream.

Margaret taught me love. She taught me to care like I'd never cared before, she taught me patience, and she taught what a home is. We were blissfully happy, we did everything together, we cycled, we went to the pub, we watched the local rugby team, we made lots of lovely friends. I hated it when I had to go away on business, and I just adored coming home.

After two years we tried to start a family, we tried and tried and much fun it was. A year then two passed, still no baby. Margaret as ever took it in her stride, "plenty of time" she said, "after all we're having fun."

And have fun we did, whilst at the same time I was getting on well in my career. Promotions came, my responsibilities grew and all the time Margaret encouraged me not to worry about her but to enjoy my work.

The clock though was ticking, six years had passed since we married, and it was my Mum who was the first outsider to ask about the prospects of a family. Time had flown, Margaret was now the supervisory Physio at the hospital and I was in charge of major contracts for my firm. The baby had somehow become an illusion for me though Margaret never stopped referring to "maybe tonight" whenever we had sex.

We were reluctant, but following Mum's prod, we started thinking hard and trying our best to get my beautiful wife pregnant. We started by planning intercourse to coincide with dates in Margaret's cycle, this went on for another year, still no luck. From then on we began to try to organise health examinations, sperm counts, x-rays, and another two years passed. Margaret now carried with her the haunted look of a mother, perhaps not to be.

On my thirtieth birthday I was invited to join the board of the company and also to buy shares, since we needed working capital for a very big contract for the Middle East. They were exciting times, busy, frenetic and demanding but the business prospects looked good. Within a year however the whole pack of cards collapsed. I was out of work with a huge mortgage and Margaret devoted all her energies to keeping my morale up as I desperately searched for a new job.

There were nights when we cried together, afraid of what tomorrow might bring. Margaret cried for the baby she seemed fated not to have and once more I was haunted by failure.

I think looking back it was me that became depressed, I couldn't afford Christmas presents and Margaret spent nights making things like chocolates and cakes which she wrapped to look as if they were from the poshest shop on the planet.

I sometimes believe that in some ways that time was the best Christmas we ever had. Despite the hard times we relied absolutely on each other, there was no one else, just us struggling, but happily together.

I've not had Christmas here yet, it has lost all its meaning now. David wants to fly me to his home in Atlanta but that seems a step too far.

Another dreadful summer, is it me? Or are British summers always awful? The sky is dull and a fine drizzle falls. Maybe I'll go out to lunch, if Geoff will come.

Sometimes I go back to my old home village, but the taxi ride is long and tortuous and I've already noted that everyone has moved on. It's getting on for a year since I fell, there are a few friends but they are getting on with their lives, I feel as if I'm an intruder, my old friends are just that; old! They're busy looking after themselves, they've all got dogs which they treat as child substitutes and I'm bound to say they aggravate me. When Johanna was alive she was a positive dynamo and organised all sorts of things from W.I. stalls, village fetes and I don't know what else. The local Pub which was the epicentre of our lives but has recently changed hands with brutal rapidity and the new people, as far as I'm concerned, are from an alien planet.

On my last visit, I Thought I'd go back and see one of my old pals, Harry Blake, I didn't ring I just escaped Swallow House in my third week, it was only my second trip out.

Harry's house was down the lane from Apple Tree Cottage which by the way was shrouded in scaffolding, the usual quiet shattered by the hammering of the philistine builders. The noise struck me like a bolt of pain. I marched with limping resolution to Harry's house.

The door opened and Doris stood there, she was dressed in an overcoat, and obviously ready to go out. She looked at me as though I'd crawled from under a rock.

"Oh John, what a surprise, look I'm sorry but I'm just on my way to the hospital, Harry's had a stroke," she was already locking the door. She turned and without breaking step marched to her car, I limped alongside.

"Is Harry all right? I'm really sorry to hear this Doris, anything I can do?"

She stopped to get into her car, hesitated for a moment. "Look I'm really sorry but I have to go." She strapped herself in started the engine, then as if in afterthought she wound down the window and called. "I'll tell him you called." Then she was gone.

Doris was never one I could warm to, even in the old days, she always behaved as if I was disreputable and Johanna was not altogether to be trusted because; a) – she was beautiful and b) – she was a foreigner. I always thought Harry was hard done by. Doris always disapproved of our gents' night out at the pub every Wednesday. We had a lot of fun and occasionally we drank too much, but we always walked home. Sometimes Harry would come home with me and have a coffee or a drop of scotch. Johanna, always the welcoming hostess, loved him and he always made a fuss of her. He was always fun, always keen to look on the good side. I think he secretly envied Apple Tree House and what a happy home it was.

On the bleak day of my ill planned visit I stood in the road, just empty and lonely. Disappointment shrouded me with a cool handed slap. 'You can't go back you old fool', what are you thinking of?

Harry has since passed away, he was younger than me by a couple of years. I didn't go to his funeral, I don't like funerals, I don't think I'll have one. No, sod it, a complete waste of money, and I have a sneaking suspicion that no one would come to it anyway.

Before I moved to Apple Tree House, Margaret continued to work in the Hospital, the days passed slowly for her, the prospect of childlessness weighed heavily on her.

I was at work again and somehow fell on my feet and was able to resurrect some of my contacts of old. Things moneywise were beginning to settle down, we even paid the mortgage each month and had a few bucks over. Once again my job wrapped me up, and now looking back, I see that I didn't focus on my lovely wife. I ignored the tired eyes, the slump in her figure, the loss of weight. As always, Margaret greeted me from my trips abroad, my late nights, and made me feel as though I was a hero, a man who was better than she deserved. Nothing, of course could have been further from the truth. I was nothing but an ambitious dim wit, who basked in success, who loved his job more than he loved his wife. I was so blind, I looked away from what was obvious. My darling girl, my beautiful Margaret was dying. Even when the chips were down, when she had to give up work, I still fooled myself that all would be well. Margaret would keep the home fires burning and I carried on from Qatar to

Canada making a 'successful' fist of the business.

Then it all came crashing down, her pain could no longer be hidden, her courage could no longer mask her agony. The medics did their best, but looking back, it was an appalling amalgam of incompetence, heroism, courage and physical waste. Margaret died horribly, she died in searing pain where her shrieks of agony echoed around the so called rest or convalescent clinic. I remember the bleakness of that awful place, cancer was known but her case was hopeless. Pain killers were administered with a frugality of such meanness as to defy logic.

I held her, a bag of shattered bones, I hushed her as she screamed and I squeezed her with all the love I had. She died with a gasp that was both ghastly and welcome. That foul pain that had possessed her had at last been exorcised. I really wished to die with her. My life was in tatters. Emptiness had a new meaning. Margaret's death had sucked the love from me, my core was empty and it hurt. I was thirty four, a limping old man on his way to an unwanted fortune.

Fifty years on, the August drizzle darkens another day, I pick up a book but I can't concentrate. Is this what life has to offer? All this blood sweat and tears, for what? 'Nothing' is in the room, 'nothing', this loneliest companion, how I hate it.

Chapter 6

David's arrival is something I look forward to. Despite my reservation about me being a damned nuisance, he's over for a week's business and then Shanta and the kids will come and David proposes that we have a few days together down in Devon.

I like to be indulged as well as the next man, but I know I am a stranger to the grandchildren and for that matter to Shanta, though she is always loving and kind to me.

I remember well when David married Shanta. Johanna and I made the pilgrimage to Chicago to meet the "in-laws". We were both apprehensive and although Shanta had charmed the boots off us, shown us many pictures of her parents there was still an apprehension about our son marrying into a different culture. I simply didn't know what to expect. Despite my international experience, including many visits to India, I was the most nervous. Johanna, as usual, not only looked lovely but shone with that Scandinavian serenity, she would love every part of the new family however it turned out. She treated me like a baby. The tables were completely overturned. Whereas I was usually the decision maker, on that journey Johanna was completely in control. Her generosity of spirit just shone through, she was open to anything that David's family were to do. If it was good enough for David it was good enough for her.

We'd met Shanta of coarse she was a lovely elegant girl, gorgeous to look at and with a most lovely voice. Whilst David had grown into a big guy Shanta was delicate beside him. She had the most gorgeous eyes and jet black shining hair, she was in short, a knock out!

David had met her through his now sophisticated social life in America where he'd become a successful senior manager in Computer development of some kind or another. David at twenty nine had the world at his feet, and Shanta seemed to be fitted to be his lovely wife.

Despite my show of being a great man of the world, I harboured a prejudice, albeit an unconscious one, whereas Johanna clearly did not. My views were very gender conscious, she was gorgeous, sure, but I had this smidgeon of reserve about her being so beautifully dark and Indian.

I'm ashamed to say I drank too much on the plane and started doing very unfortunate Indian impersonations drawn from dreadful UK TV programmes. I waved my arms and hands, muttering absurdities. What started as a mildly humorous joke turned into rather bad taste and Johanna got cross and insisted the attendant served me no more booze.

"What, what, what, you are saying I'm pissed, whut, whut, whaat!"

"You are behaving like a child. Have a nap and shut up, I don't want the children meeting a drunken old man, who is plainly a lousy comedian and a racist to boot! And you, excuse me," she caught the eye of the airhostess, "my husband is the little the worse for wear, no more alcohol please."

The pretty airhostess added to my humiliation, "You naughty boy." I thought for one dreadful moment she was going to tussle my 68year old head.

For Johanna to be cross was a rare thing. We generally got on extremely well, whenever we disagreed she had a way of absolving us from mutual blame. At worst she would say, "OK let's think about it." It was a polite way of saying "be quiet" but it always worked.

Johanna's Dad was arriving on the next day as was Jenni and a host of assorted relations. As I sank into my guilt filled reverie, I couldn't help the anxiety returning. What if, this or that? I could have done with another drink but that was not to be.

David and Shanta met us at the Airport, and I was immediately ashamed of my hapless performance. Shanta gave me a hug, which was at once delicate, warm, feminine and welcoming. What a lucky boy David was. We were driven to our hotel about half an hour from the airport. In our lovely suite there were at least four huge bouquets of flowers welcoming us.

A note and bottle of Champagne on the table declared a warm welcome from Ashmaan and Aanya Roy, Shanta's mum and dad.

The next days were a blur of such rich hospitality and colour, we were swept away into such delight as I have never or since experienced. It was not just the extravagance of it all, it was the reality of the heart felt welcome. The ceremony itself was magnificent, but at the same time holy, sincere, heart to heart. Both

Johanna and I agreed that if there is a God, he was there.

The culture was different, I was right about that, it was like being wrapped in a blanket of love. Dr. Ashmaan Roy was the perfect host, he greeted Jenni my sister as if he had known her all is life, he obviously had taken David to his heart and both he and Aanya positively gloated on our boy. We were included in everything including a meeting with the officiant an Indian elder, with a wonderful twinkle in his eyes. We were shown around the massive marquee set up like a palace in their garden. It was mind bogglingly opulent, like a fairy tale from the exotic east.

The ceremony itself was fantastic and we were included into its heart. I still remember the sentiments of the vows that David and Shanta exchanged, they are a lesson for us all. There were seven steps as they walked around a flame and the last vow was more or less as follows:

David's vow: "Oh friends! allow us to cover the seventh step together, this promise, our Saptapad-friendship. Please be my constant wife."

Shanta's vow: "Yes, today, I gained you, I secured the highest kind of friendship with you. I will remember the vows we just took and adore you forever sincerely with all my heart."

By now both Johanna and I were in floods of tears.

Much water has passed under the bridge since then and I am so happy that David and Shanta are still together and have two lovely kids. Their life seems a joy, I just hope I don't get in the way of all that happiness.

It's a week before they come, so I must get myself up to speed. That means being as fit as I can, being organised and trying very hard to convince them both that I am happily ensconced in Swallow House.

Chapter 7

It is the second Thursday in the month, it is eleven o clock and in Swallow House that means I must go down to 'the Lockup' for doctor or nurse's visit.

"Mr. Betts, and how are you today?" I am greeted by a quite attractive nurse in her crisp blue uniform. Her blonde hair is tied severely in a bun at the back of her pretty head. She smiles, I'm not sure if she's really smiling or grimacing at another old codger she is forced to deal with.

"Fine thank you, never been better." I reply, my cheeks locked into a grimace I hope passes for a smile.

"How's your leg? Settling down I hope."

'Settling down, what is she talking about?' I've had this gammy leg for sixty five years and it has always been a pain, both literally and actually. Of course falling down the stairs hardly helped.

"Bit stiff I suppose. Only stiff thing about me."
An unfortunate sexual innuendo I fancy, but she
lets it pass without a second's thought.

"Let's have a look at your ankle, cumm'on Mr
Betts let's get you on the bed."

I hop up as best as any eighty four year old can
hop, and manoeuvre myself so that my ankle is
raised. The nurse whose name is Margaret
Pleasance according to her badge. "Margaret
Pleasance, Sister. – Bupa".

She removes my shoe and sock and reveals my
deformed ankle. It is unpleasant to the eye.
Lumpy, swollen and with several scars, my foot
below looks as if belongs to a cadaver. It is
white, skinny with horrid toe nails. What a very
unpleasant job Sister Margaret has.

"I hope you're paid reasonably well." I regret
the comment immediately.

Margaret replies very matter of factly, "Better
than in the Health Service I must say but I do

feel a guilt sometimes, I was a theatre sister, but I quit and did a bit of repping for a while for a drug company, quite enjoyed that but I was away from the kids and Dave too much so here I am looking after my favourite patients." She looked up and smiled.

How nice she is, this Sister Margaret. Her soft hand rub moisturiser over my hapless ankle, and it is heavenly. "Oh, that's so nice."

"Good," she says, "you need your feet doing, I'll arrange the chiropodist to call, and I think a physio to help you with your leg. It's very immobile."

"Need a bike, that's about the only exercise that works, the joint hasn't rotated for years - worse now I suppose, but there we are, rugby and alcohol."

The Sister laughs. Puts back my shoe and sock, and my visit is coming to an end. I suddenly feel I don't want to go back to my rooms, I want to talk to Sister Margaret, I want to take her to lunch.

"Everything else seems fine, your blood pressure is good, and weight stable we'll see again in a month."

I mutter a sad thank you, pick up my stick and as sedately as I can, withdraw.

Margaret, Margaret, I didn't see you fade, I did, but I didn't want to see what was in front of me. The prospect of children had faded, we'd talked briefly of the idea of adopting. But by the time of our first crisis and my second ascent to reasonable success I was concentrated on me, me myself and I. Margaret held the fort, hid her suffering and gave of herself without thought. I was clambering up the business pole whilst the girl I loved began to die and I just didn't bother to look at what was before my very eyes.

I shut the door and put on the kettle, I am crying again, mourning that lovely girl who died for me forty years ago.

There's a knock on the door,

"Come in!" It's Joan the sexy commandant matron.

"Mr Betts, sister says you're in good health but we have to keep an eye on your leg." She held her elbows as if I were going to attack her, at the same time she's looking round to see if I've done something frightful, made a mess or been at the scotch before lunch.

"Bugger off Joan, I'm fine and I have enough sense to let you know if I need any help, medical or otherwise."

"Now, John watch your language there's a good man, we always look after our folk, we care about you John."

I sigh, I don't want to talk to Joan. Despite her smart appearance there's something about her I don't like, I have no idea, but it may be her authority, her smarty arse 'I'm in charge' aura. She's just too bossy, I'm too old to take orders, I wish she'd bugger off.

"Forgive me Joan, I've got things to do."

The door closed behind her, there was a muffled noise from the corridor, I filled my tea cup and topped the dark tea with a large scotch. 'Nothing' stalks the room.

'Don't be so miserable John, Sister Margaret, she's very sweet, and I know she reminded you of me. Be a good boy now, we were happy you know, I know we didn't have the child we wanted, but we loved each other – didn't we?' Margaret's eyes are filled with tears, "I was proud of you, you worked so hard, and you held me when I was ill, oh! How I loved you, I hated saying goodbye even if I didn't know what I was saying through all that pain. One thing, John that made it tolerable, even beautiful, was that

we loved each other, never forget that John, never.."

The noise outside is louder, what's going on? I open the door and I see Dan being wheeled off to the lockup. Well, I suppose it was inevitable. I hope Geoff is free for a chat, that 'nothing' is too close for comfort. I have second thoughts, I feel sorry about Dan, poor man has done nothing to hurt me yet I've been impatient and rude. Now he's failing, I feel a shit, a nasty grumbling miserable old shit.

What if something happens to Geoff? I'll have no one to talk to or have a beer with, maybe I'll be next off to the lockup. How do I feel? Pretty good actually, I get tired a bit and my gammy leg hurts but then it always has. I dare not doze because I know I'll think about Dan, poor bugger. I expect that Mr. Bloody Boyd, the bishop of Swallow House will be waving the good book about and ministering to dear old Dan as he inevitably looks forward to his exit from this home for the hopeless.

I cannot do this mooning about in my rooms, after lunch I shall go out. No idea where or who with, but out I shall go and make sure 'nothing' doesn't monopolise my day.

I don't know what I've done to deserve this but Bishop Boyd is the only man at lunch, Dan of course is in the lockup, apparently had a stroke this morning, Geoff has a chill and is confined to his room.

"What ho! Boyd." I'm as jolly as I can be, "sorry to see Dan unwell. Still poor old bugger hasn't been in top form since I've been here."

"Indeed Dan has succumbed to a stroke, I have had the opportunity to visit him briefly, sadly, he is barely conscious." He devoured his bread roll as if were to be his last.

 I tried hard to stay attentive, after all I'm running out of chums.

"I know that spiritually speaking that Dan will have gathered some strength from my visit, and hopefully this will help his recovery."

'Bollocks' I said but under my breath, what a sanctimonious twit Boyd is. "Is he to remain in the lockup or are they taking him to the hospital?"

Much of the excellent tomato and basil soup has been spilled down the bishop's shirt, he is I assume unconscious of this, the cross he wears is smeared with the reddish soup, his purple shirt blotched as if with blood. I muse that this may be a premonition of things to come, maybe I'll murder the boring old bugger.

"I do wish you wouldn't use that term, 'the lockup' you know it's the medical facility and we have excellent care, so whatever is decided I'm sure Dan will receive the best of care." He ladled what is left of his soup up with a quiet but lengthy slurp, yet another drop drips and reduces the holy man to the short fat, silly old man that he is.

The lunch passes slowly, Boyd talks of his apparently distinguished past as a clergyman and academic. He can't fool me, I know a joker when I see one and he fits the bill to a tee. I skip coffee, go to my room, pick up my wallet and march out as smartly as I can dragging the gammy leg with me. After rushing and omitting to signing out I have no idea where I'm going, so I stand at the bus stop outside Swallow House.

Chapter 8

The bus is empty except for two loutish youths who sit near the front of the single decker. The driver is bemused by my offer of a ten pound note and made me sit down after shovelling the tenner back to me. The foul mouthed and scruffy youths sprawl, one with his feet across the gap and onto the seat opposite, I don't know why, but I stand in front of them and with my walking stick gently waving to suggest he put his feet on to floor.

"Perhaps it might be more considerate to other passengers if you put your feet on the floor."

"What you sayin', whatsit to you, you old git? Why don't you fuck off before you fall down grandpa?"

Perplexed, I stood my ground for about a second, then I took their advice and sat. I felt humiliated, I wanted to get up and give them a damned good hiding with my stick. Maybe it was a good idea, then again maybe it wasn't.

At the next stop, the youths got up to go, the taller one looked at me and sneered, "You need to be careful grandpa, or someone could give you a fucking hidin', you know wha' I mean, eh?" Then, amidst a roar of hysterical laughter, they were gone.

At the town centre, the sun came to greet my unsure steps. Before me, a half empty car park and looming over me a Kentucky Fried Chicken and the Co-op. I had only been here a few times over the years, and the ugliness of the place made me feel unsettled. For years I had lived like a toff, studiously avoiding the ordinary and the ugly, yet this town was a home to thousands, this was the centre for hundreds of families young and old. No Apple Tree Cottages here, just run down shops, and as I walked on, not many of them. The Star and Garter had seen better days, the Charity shops needed a coat of paint and a few stall holders lined the pavement. As far as I could see they sold vegetables or junk, by junk I mean things I didn't have a need for, like phones and music gadgets.

Bleedin' Boyd has a lot to answer for, I made an unplanned escape, but to where? To this dreadful town, which has absolutely nothing to offer at least as far as I can see. My leg is hurting so I pop into the 'Star and Garter', on the step at the entrance there is a spilled metal ashtray. I nudge over it, my confidence ebbing away – What am I doing here? The place smells of ale and faintly of disinfectant, the floor is wooden and the walls a curious off yellow as though they'd been smoking here without a break for ever.

Behind the bar, a huge man in shirtsleeves smiles at me as if I was his pal, "What can I get you? Sir" his voice is a surprise, light and quite cultured. The bar is busier than I expected, there must be twenty people here, gathered in groups of two and three. I am the only man who is alone.

"A pint of your best bitter will be fine, how much is that?"

It costs a surprisingly small amount, and it looks a treat, foaming with a light head and the beer soon settles as clear as a bell. There is nowhere vacant to sit so I perch on the end of a table where two middle aged men are engrossed in conversation. As soon as I sit they stop talking. The older grisly guy eyes me, he hasn't shaved for a week, his shirt is open at the neck, his smart flat cap is at a jaunty angle, and his pullover reminds me of one my father used to wear way back in the war. In a shambolic way he is jaunty smart.

Despite his appearance I'm surprised as he smiles at me, his smile shows an absence of at least a quarter of his teeth.

"A'ter noon, how d'y do, haven't seen you 'ere before." His broad West Country accent is quite difficult to understand, it takes a second to translate.I feel my momentary stare, as his message sinks in, is taken amiss.

"Oh, sorry old boy, not surprising really, haven't been here before. Nice beer," I take a self-conscious slurp.

"We come down 'ere all the time don' we Dave, this is Dave I'm Terry."

"Oh, I'm John, nice to meet you."

"Well John, what d'ya think of the 4:30, Wincanton, 'Marge's Might', Dave says it's a cert don' ya Dave?"

"Not sure, not my thing really, don't gamble, you see." I heard myself and I sounded such a buffoon, like some sort of hooray Henry from another planet.

Dave, his head suddenly protruding round Terry, "Bleedin' cert could be as much as fifteen to one." He tapped his nose, "got my sources John." He swallowed the rest of his pint.

"Fancy another pint do you John?" says Terry, picking up his and Dave's empty glasses.

"No thanks, I've hardly got into this one yet, though it is very nice.

"Go on John have one on us, we don't see many newcomers in 'ere do we Dave?"

"Right," says Dave. Dave is younger than Terry, he wears jeans and a denim shirt, his forearms are covered in tattoos, and he needs a haircut. His shoes need a clean, but I note his hands are immaculate, except for the huge and rather vulgar rings on his fingers. He wears an enormous watch.

Terry sidles up the bench to my end of the table. "We're just havin' a few, cos we're waitin' for the last races, we've bagged a couple but the 4:30 our big chance,.. you sayin' you don't dabble then John?"

"Dabble?, Sorry, I don't understand."

"Back the horses John, have a tickle now and again, you know." He smiles at me as though he's about to pick my pocket. I get the uneasy feeling I'm in the wrong place at the wrong time. His cap I notice looks really new, expensive, I'm getting confused, I'm very uncomfortable. I feel threatened, I am afraid.

Dave plonks three pints of beer on the table. "There you go John, one for the road." Terry swallows a great gulp from his new pint as does Dave. I have not yet finished my first one. I wonder, how do I escape?

"How old are you John?" Terry looks quizzically over his pint.

My first responsive thought is to tell him to mind his business but I relent.

"Eighty four, getting a bit long in the tooth, don't you know!"

"Same age as my Dad," says Terry, "How old's your Dad Dave?"

"I dunno, 'bout seventy four I reckon."

"My Dad doesn't look 'alf as good as you John, he's in an 'ome."

"So am I."

"In a bleedin' 'ome, you're kidding me aren't you? Got any kids have ya?"

I need to think, Terry is too much for me, I feel I'm being overwhelmed, swept up by a couple of ne'r-do-wells. I swallow my first pint, what's left of it.

"I have a son, he's in America."

"Doin' well is he? My boys are both in the business."

Probably some shady business I think. I don't respond, I'm going to drink the second pint and then make myself scarce. The questions keep coming, I slow down, 'think, you old bugger, think'!

"He's doing well, cyber engineering and all that." That's got them, another mouthful of beer. Much to my amazement Terry and Dave continue the conversation. Terry goes into some detail about cyber engineering and applications from information technology and robotics to automobile cyber systems of the future. I am almost dumb with surprise. I am lost for words.

"If you've got some cash to spare John, I can make you a few quid, fancy that, do ya?"

Here comes the con trick, I'm not that stupid. These chaps must think I'm some half-witted old fart. Let me get rid of this pint and I'm out of here.

"Look John, I don't want anything from you mate, it's just that I can't go into the first betting shop with a £200 bet, because he'll flag it up to the other shops see?"

"No, I don't see and I'm afraid I'm going to go straight home so I can't help you." I say this in a positive but neutral way. I am unsure about these men, it's as if I've been propositioned by someone up to no good, in fact I believe that's definitely the case. I must escape.

"Do me a favour John," implores Dave, "Look here's two hundred quid, put the bet on for me, and we'll come back and we'll have a drink and you can wait for your commission. What's wrong with that, eh?"

The beer is beginning to make me less sure of myself, "What commission?" I enquire, I feel the tiniest slur in "commission".

"Depends on the odds John, but say the stake, two hundred quid, how's that?"

I am astonished, two hundred pounds is not a lot of money in the great picture of things, but two hundred pounds for no risk and two minutes work seems somehow surreal and not without its excitement. Dave seems not that bothered really, he's seems very relaxed, certainly more than I am.

"Are you serious? You barely know me, maybe I'll bugger off with your money, jump on a bus and never be seen again." I'm nearly down to the bottom of my second pint.

"What do you think Terry? Do you think John will run away with my two hundred quid, eh Terry?"

"My Dad wouldn't that's for sure, neither will John he's a bit of a toff."

At which point Dave pressed ten twenty pound notes into my hand, "John do us a favour, you're a nice bloke, it'll be a pleasure to work wi' thee."

And so I began to work with Dave and Terry, who apart from being full time gamblers, I found to be delightful company. Despite their curious dress sense, they were worldly, well-educated and absolutely straightforward with me. I learned that they worked in a syndicate where information was the key. I had no idea where the leads came from, apparently Dave and Terry worked the West Country, or so they told me and had maximum budgets, that is to say, they agreed limits on their bets so as not to scare the casino/betting houses. They didn't always win, but they always moved from town to town and generally made a very good living indeed. They would allow me to be their courier, and help with occasional appearances in towns within a reasonable distance of my base.

"That seems straight forward, are you sure this is all legal?"

"Sure John," nothing for you to worry about mate. Dave holds my upper arm firmly, almost with affection.

That night, I arrived back at Swallow House by taxi, clutching two bottles of premium whiskey which I'd planned to secrete away in my rooms.

Jane McCann saw me arrive, and appeared at my room door waiting like a Gestapo princess.

"Mr Betts, John, you know we like to know when and where you're off to especially when you're on your own, and you didn't sign out this afternoon, it's now half passed seven and we were worried about you."

I stood there feeling a little bit the worse for wear, I'd had three pints of bitter and a couple of scotches with my new pals, Terry and Dave. I had my supermarket bag in my hand and my full attention was focussed on not rattling its contents. However it would be impossible to put the bag down since I had to find my key and of course my walking stick was the other key accoutrement. If I leaned the stick against the wall I knew it would slide, if I put the bag down the bottles would clank. I hoped vainly that I was not swaying too much.

"Forgive me dear lady but I must go to the loo, forgive my haste." Ms. McCann did not retreat.

She stared at me, I stared back. Much to my relief, after an impasse that seemed an eternity she turned on her heel and I was safe with my booty.

Chapter 9

Secreting away my stash of scotch, was more difficult than I had imagined. Although my rooms were spacious, they were ordered, every suite was much the same although I had brought my own Victorian desk. I had keys for this particular piece of furniture and so after much thought I put the contraband bottles in the lower drawer. It's one of my few hiding places. With that, and the rigours of the day I went to bed and slept like a top.

I was awoken by Alex, much later than usual, and my mild hangover was made much the worse as I heard him rooting about in my desk, which it transpired I had left open before I went to bed. I rumbled out of bed and limped into the living room where Alex stood over the desk, the bottles standing plainly for all to see from the open bottom draw.

Alex his arms folded, looked at me and he moved to point at the offending cache, "Mr. Betts, presents for someone are they?"

"Yes, they are, bugger off Alex."

"Sorry John, but Ms. McCann spotted your... uhm... uhm imports, I'll have to take one bottle away, you know the rules, one bottle of each spirit max per week, let's see what you've got shall we?"

"Piss off Alex," I was cross.

"Excuse me Mr. Betts but there's a bird hanging out of its cage." He pointed at my limp appendage peeping from my pyjamas.

My humiliation complete, I turned back to my bedroom incandescent with rage. I shall leave this barracks for the demented, I shall bugger off and get a flat somewhere. I dress with haste which of course takes me longer than ever, I can't get this bloody shoe on. I have not yet noted the weather, I am nevertheless dressed in my blazer complete with regimental tie, I shall lay into that bossy bitch McCann and get the hell out of this Swallow Hole, this jail!

Half an hour has passed, Ms McCann has me seated in her business-like office. It has the mix between a sales office with plush chairs for the punters and the headmasters study. McCann sits, composed, not a hair out of place, smugly looking at me as if I'm some sort of mental defective. She has said very little since I told her what I really thought of her bullying ways and the boarding school rules of her dreadful establishment. There is a silence, McCann drinks her coffee slowly I have already gulped mine down, I resist the urge to burp.

"Well dear Mr Betts, John, I'm sorry to see you so upset," she smiles, her made up face shows tiny cracks where the makeup cakes round her cold but smiling eyes, "John, we really care for you here, not because we have to, but because we want to,.. you're a valued member of our little community. I can understand your aggravation but Alex was only doing his duty. You know that we have to have some discipline John, the same for everyone."

The air hangs heavy. I stare back at her, "Jesus, woman, I'm eighty bloody four, I'm not a child, I don't pay a fortune to be followed round like some demented adolescent."

"John, I know that and all the staff respect that, it's just that we need to have some rules here or it would be anarchy. You can always have a drink down stairs in the conservatory, any time you like, you know that, but we have pledged to look after you to David, you know he cares for you very much."

"Bollocks, he wants me tethered so he can get on with his life……. I can see his point, but I think I ought to leave and get a little flat somewhere and not be a nuisance." I suddenly feel very sorry for myself, what a pathetic performance.

"I'll make arrangements to leave, please arrange my bill and I'll get out of your hair."

McCann shifts in her chair. "Look John, please think……. I hate to say this but you know David wants you to be safe, and …and he has the power of attorney and if you really do wish to leave you'll have to clear it with him, John I don't want to have to ring him, …. Just think about your plans, please."

The red mist starts to rise, David will do something spectacular like ship me to America which is the last thing I want. I'll have to think this through, I have to look beyond my own temper and see what I really want. Which is? I have no idea! It may be better if I die, get the hell out of this school for ancients and not be a bloody nuisance. McCann really aggravates me but I don't know why. Maybe it's because she's young and smart. Is it because she's the boss, the headmistress, the keeper of the keys? How do I save face here? I am bewildered, I have nowhere to go, I am not free, from my gammy leg or this prison. I feel I want to cry – fuck it, perhaps I should top myself. I don't know what to say.

"David's coming over next week, perhaps we could get together and all see what's best. Now John, please take your time, we'll do anything we can to help you get over this…how shall we say?....upset."

I get up to go, like a small boy who has been reprimanded, but I know the problem, it's me, I'm a useless old bugger. I stumble back to my rooms and search out my last hidden bottle of single malt. Victory of a sort I suppose. It's only eleven in the morning, steady as she goes. The one malt warms me as it slips down.

There's a knock on the door. It's Geoff, he is, as always smiling.

"New boys arriving," he announces, "fresh blood, old boy." their rooms are being made ready, "Dan must still be with us his place remains untouched."

I must say the news bucks me up. New faces will be a good thing, and I will be able to get out more often with Terry and Dave, all being well. I haven't mentioned my new 'consultancy' to McCann yet, or to anyone else for that matter. I must plan, or that awful woman will conspire to get in my way. The prospect of a new 'job' and new faces definitely cheers me up. (What I must do now is create a scenario where my new job with the Terry and Dave outfit sounds orthodox.) A challenge, I fancy!

"I'm thinking of going back to work Geoff, what do you think?"

Geoff, as usual replies after an interminable gap. "You Serious?"

"Absolutely old boy, I have an old chum who's doing market research – interested in the mature persons market."

"And what pray, are you going to do?"

"They want me to go round small towns and give my impressions of the shopping from a mature person's stand point."

"Good heavens, I didn't think anyone was interested in that sort of thing, sounds jolly interesting. Will you get paid?"

"Not much, but it will get me out, they provide transport and expenses, anyway we'll see."

"Fancy a beer? Geoff,?"

We sign the book and see one of our new colleagues, he has his children with him they are both in their sixties I would say. He has the sad look of a man being sent away to school and he knows he's never going to get released. The man is tall, lean and straight. I get the immediate impression that he's a military type. His face is skinny and at first looks severe but when he sees us he smiles.

Geoff without hesitation goes across and greets our new friend.

"Don't want to presume anything, but John and me, I'm Geoff by the way Professor Geoff Watkins and this is John Betts." He acknowledges the new man's offspring, they smile relieved that the tension around locking their old man up is somehow eased. They smile, you can almost hear the intake of relieving breath.

"What ho!" say I rather pathetically. "We're just popping out for a pint, spot of lunch…"

Everyone smiles. Henry, that's the new man's name, says, "See you later," and in they go. I catch site of the dreaded McCann bosom forward, smile of welcome ablaze. I make a beeline for the taxi.

That fateful day was just the beginning, three more inmates arrived in quick order. Apart from Henry, retired Colonel, there came Nigel, Simon and Brian. They were all in their eighties and all very different, in remarkable ways. Henry turned out to be a good sport and was what I remember as a piss artist, that means he drank alcohol with a relish and whenever he had a chance. Nigel was a quieter fellow and immediately got on with Geoff which annoyed me at first but then Henry and I seemed to team up. Simon assumed dear old Dan's role of the fading invalid, complete with wheelchair and a limp mind. To be fair he seemed a bit gha-gha and I prophesied that he would go almost immediately to the lock-up and so it transpired. Brian was entirely different if you get my drift, he was what we used to call queer, now I believe, we have to use the word gay.

Despite Brian's obvious peculiarities, he was a delightful fellow and was a big hit with the ladies. He was a complete fop, always had a kerchief hanging from his breast pocket. He paraded his gayness, and swaggered about making great theatrical bows and arm waves as he chassied through the public rooms. He called everyone 'darling' except Henry, he seemed to know when to draw the line. He called Boyd, 'Bishop, darling, which delighted at least me. Boyd though to his everlasting credit stopped wincing after about a month. Boyd by the way was still a cause of great annoyance, but the other boys seemed to put up with his pompous nonsense.

Henry was first a bit grumpy about Brian, but Brian too was not averse to a contraband bottle or two and it was not long before, me, the Colonel and Brian started having really comfortable chats in our quarters. McCann was on to us in a nono-second. We spent much of September playing a sophisticated game of 'hide the booze'.

McCann's cunning response was to call more evening parties, called residents' evenings when both male and female 'guests' were encouraged to mix with a cocktail in hand, and then play bridge or watch a movie. Sometimes the evenings were spiced up by the presence of a few married couples. I tried hard to convince myself that theses younger ladies were seeking the company of more distinguished older men. The delusion didn't last long. Up until now I had studiously avoided these old fart junkets, but with Henry's encouragement I acquiesced.

It was at one of these evenings, in late September, the swallows had suddenly flown away. That made me a bit sad and I wondered how many more times, if any, I would see my little friends swooping in the grounds.

I digress. Brian and I had escaped after a movie and went his room. After dispensing two generous scotches, Brian began to show me the photographs of his past. He'd been the editor of several well-known magazines and something of a celebrity in the worlds of theatre and fashion.

At first I will admit to a certain discomfort, but considering our combined age of one hundred and sixty five, this seems disingenuous to say the least.

"Brian," I moaned, "I find this place OK but you know I find it hard to leave my life behind."

"Awe, you mustn't darling, I bet you had a great life, we're having a little drinkie, aren't we, I think you're a lovely man who's accomplished a lot and I think I'm lucky, darling, to have met you and Henry and even that silly bugger Boyd. So don't go feeling sorry for yourself, there's lots worse off than us."

He was quite right of course.

I couldn't resist telling him about my girls, Margaret and Johanna, how much I loved them both, and how much I missed them.

Brain responded, "I miss my Brendan darling, forty two years we were together, he was such a lovely man. I know you old straight buggers think we're all perverts and so on, but Brendan and me we loved each other as surely as the sun comes up each morning and as surely as it goes down each night. Brendan was younger than me, he left his wife and a kid, to live with me. He was the sweetest man ever, he loved me and he loved his son, I think he loved his wife too, but anyway she went off a couple of years after we got together and that was that. He always kept in touch with his boy though. His funeral was massive and his son and I were the main mourners. I felt so proud having Jonathan at me side, he was a smashing lad."

At this point he started crying, I didn't know what to do so without thought I held his hand, my tears barely contained.

"There you are John, you're a kind nice man, I know we both weep, for different people but we're all the same, aren't we darling."

I rose from my chair, having learned a great lesson, I had a new friend.

Chapter 10

"Dan would like to see you." It was the dreaded Boyd.

"Dan! Wants to see me? Whatever for?"

"Yes, he wishes to see you, be kind there's a good man. Dan isn't very well I'm afraid. He's in Room two in the medical wing."

I was confused, dear old Dan as I considered him now, as he was, as it were, no longer with us, was someone who I hardly knew and had hitherto judged him as a doddering nuisance. It is true that I've modified my view probably because Dan is out of sight and out of mind. What can he possibly want?

Boyd fixed me with his 'holier than thou' look.

"OK, I'll arrange to go and see him, perhaps tomorrow."

"It would be better if you went now." Boyd was almost sinister.

"Very well," I was somehow cowed by the weight of his reverence, I must be getting even more senile.

Room 2 in the medical wing was just like any private hospital ward anywhere, perhaps a bit more luxurious. Dan was attached to all manner of contraptions and the monitor that hooted a continuous bleep.

"What oh! old chap," was all I could think to say.

Dan's thin silver hair was just visible above the oxygen mask his eyebrows twitched, and his meagre hand waved toward the bedside chair. A nurse I had never seen before bade me sit and told me I could have ten minutes with my "Friend". She pointed to the emergency button and swished out of the room.

I must say Dan's voice had not improved or maybe my hearing had gone south but I could only see him whispering, not hear a word. Bugger! Nothing has changed really.

"You don't like me do you?" My ear is pressed close to Dan's whispering mask.

"Don't know about that Dan, don't really know each other, do we?"

There's more muttering and I have to press my ear to Dan's steaming mask,

"Do me a favour, please there's a good man will you?"

"Surely if I can, ask away old boy."

"Grab the pillow and stick it over my head until I stop moving, I want to go now and you can help me on my way."

"Fuck! Dan you can't be serious, I can't do that, no! no! no! no! no! no, goodness gracious no! I can't do that." I am shaking, Dan's pale blue eyes stare at me, his cold hand reaches for mine but I withdraw it.

"Look, Dan,…. I know that you're not well but things might get better, and in any case I could never do what you ask, it's not just in me to do such a thing."

Dan surges an inch toward me, "I thought you had guts, but you're just like Boyd full of hot air." He collapsed back onto his pillow clearly exhausted. He looks terrified and in confusion. I feel desperately sorry for him, I suddenly want to cry again. Jesus what's wrong with me, I'm bursting into tears at the drop of a hat. I swallow, try and get myself together. Dan is dying and he wants to die now.

"Ok, Ok, you sure you want this?" Christ what am I saying? Dan nods, "please," he hisses.

I pick up his pillow he flops backwards, I am shaking like a leaf. "You sure, Dan?" I hoped in that second he would recant. "Yes," He nods, I can barely hear his soft but clear whisper.

I pull the pillow free and bring it up over Dan's face.

"Ten minutes up!" The smart little nurse breezes back into the ward. I puff up the pillow and raise Dan's head,… "Making him a bit more comfortable." I mumble.

"That's kind." She says, "Here! let me do that."

I turned and as fast as my gammy leg will carry me I scamper from Dan's last stand, I am still shaking like a leaf. My heart is hammering away, I am perspiring and almost gasping for breath, God dammit, Dan has nearly killed the wrong man.

I speed out of the 'lockup' and take the elevator to my floor, I hope desperately that no one can see me. I feel as if I'm about to burst, my heart is still hammering away. I was so close to committing murder, Jesus what was I thinking of.

Colonel Henry almost bumps into me as I emerge from the lift.

"Good God old boy what's up, you look as if you've seen a ghost."

I try to slip past him but he will have none of it and follows me back to my room, perhaps follow is wrong, he escorts me, he obviously expects my imminent collapse. The way I feel now he may well be right. At my door |I fiddle with my card key, "Here old boy, let me." Henry is taking charge.

"Come on old boy, sit yourself down, I'll put on the kettle."

I do as I am told, panic still rises in my throat, I think I'm going to be sick.

"Want to share old bean? Problem shared is a problem halved, what?."

"I just tried to murder Dan." I sob uncontrollably, "Jesus, I would have done it if the nurse had not come in." I sob some more, I can hardly get my breath.

Henry stands, as upright as ever, "Don't talk bollocks, John. You must have that wrong. Tell me what happened." He hands me a glass of scotch, hurriedly dispensed.

It all rushes out of me the whole wretched tale, I have no explanation why on earth I would even contemplate doing Dan's bidding. I barely know the man for God's sake. But something from somewhere almost most compelled me to do the most awful thing.

"Look you didn't murder anyone, you may have thought about helping poor old Dan to exit this life, but you didn't. Period! You didn't John and I don't believe for one moment you'd have gone through with it."

"I don't know, Dan is in the most awful torment, I don't know if he's in pain or just lost in a sea of confusion, but whatever it is, he's had enough, poor sod. If he was a horse we'd put him down. There's part of me which is ashamed of prevaricating, if I'd not hesitated I'd have done what he wanted before the nurse came back. I think he really wanted me to do it. Bugger! Why did he choose me of all people?"

"John, let's go out. But first you are not to tell anyone, anyone." "Understood?"

"Understood."

 I gathered up my wallet and Henry signed the book 'out to lunch' and off we went to 'the Dog and Doublet.' Still very shaken I sat and ordered a large scotch which Henry countermanded with a half of bitter.

"No good getting plastered old boy, need to keep yourself together, what?"

We sat in silence and eventually I began to feel more composed, I thought of poor old Dan panicking and striving for peace with no one to help him. How bleak, how awful, how so very bloody sad.

"Settle down old boy, awful experience for you, you must not hold yourself in any blame, it was unreasonable of Dan to ask you to do that terrible thing. Good thing you hesitated, really awful… what do you want for lunch?"

"Poor old Dan, he has nowhere to go but out the door, and the only way is down a dreadful road. Poor bugger, if was a dog we'd put him down. How do you think we'll be?"

"Who knows, I saw young men die when I was a young Officer in Malaya, and then again in Korea, and then again in the Falklands. None of them deserved to die and none of them died easily, I'm battle hardened I suppose. I'll never forget one of them, old lovely boys, all of them like brothers whether other ranks or officers, all lovely boys. Didn't matter if I was a Subaltern or a Colonel I still grieved, we all did. Then I lost my wife, like you, and we grieved a different grief."

"I'll have a beef sandwich on brown." Suddenly I didn't want to think about Dan, or Johanna, or death. Death stood, a dark shadow in the pub doorway. I knew perhaps for the first time that 'nothing' was the harbinger of my end.. How will it be? I shuddered, "I'll have another half of bitter, if I may?"

"Of course old boy, let's talk about something more cheerful shall we? When is your boy coming to see you?"

Despite Henry's kindness I found it hard to shake off the horror of my morning's encounter with Dan. A mixture of regret and fear combined to bring back the realisation that we old buggers are queueing up to die. I also feel that I've let Dan down, the old man as I used to perceive him, is now etched into my psyche, a man at once brave and deserving, a man who I'd let down in the most important moment of our lives.

Back at my room, I find it impossible to shake off my depression. 'Nothing' crowds in, even the prospect of my son's and his family's visit, can't get 'nothing' out of my echoing mind.

I make up my mind to go down to the lockup and see if I can do anything for Dan. Do what? I have no idea. I trudge down in the late afternoon, 'nothing' still shrouds around me, it is the coldest my heart has ever been. All I know is, - I know nothing – but maybe I can help Dan. Kill him? Comfort him?

The pretty nurse is sitting at the entrance to the wards. She looks up and immediately rises as I came in.

"I'm sorry Mr Betts, your friend passed about an hour ago." She lays a friendly hand on my arm. "He was peaceful, his family have been informed."

'Nothing' scored another resounding victory, I turn on my heel, I am not sad I am relieved that Dan has gone. He's gone and asked nothing of me, good old Dan. Sod it, I barely knew the man. And yet I grieve.

Chapter 11

David, Shanta and the kids really lightened my
mood. Their arrival is noisy and good natured,
Shanta, as always, shines with her great looks,
glossy hair and sheer feminine beauty. She is
older, fuller, more beautiful than ever. The
children had grown unbelievably since I had last
seen them into strapping teenagers. Their arrival
is a shot in the arm and a chance to break out of
Swallow House.

"How are you Dad, you really look well."
David hugs me almost crushing the wind out of
me.

"So lovely to see you." A gentle and perfumed
embrace from my gorgeous daughter in law.

"Hi Gramps", it's a self-conscious, American
drawl from the kids.

"Wonderful to see you all." I mean it, it really is.

The only fly in the ointment is our meeting with the dreaded McCann which is inescapable. However, she is all sweetness and light.

"How lovely to see you." Oozes the meticulous McCann.

By an unseen, unspoken agreement neither of us mentions my outburst about shoving off to independence. David I think notices the tension but chooses to ignore it.

McCann immaculate as ever, continues smoothly into the delight of having me as one of her most popular guests, which is bollocks. She moves smoothly on reporting on my health which is apparently "absolutely outstanding" for a man of my age.

"John, has a lovely bunch of friends, don't you John?"

Like an uncertain schoolboy I mutter my assent.

"We're so happy that Dad has settled so well, he's just flourishing here, aren't you Dad?"

Again I mumble my agreement, what do they know anyway? I can't wait to get out of Miss Smartarse's office. I put on my best beaming smile.

There follows a discreet discussion about my financial affairs and the outrageous fees of this hollow prison for the expiring. I grin, knowing that my resources like everyone else here, are at least comfortable, indeed more than that.

The kids' arrival and the subsequent release from the dreaded McCann is a huge episode of excitement,. A massive high, all my doubts are banished, it is truly wonderful to see them, to touch them, to sense them as tangible real loving parts of me.

Two days on the South Coast though begin to take its toll, suddenly the grandchildren are too busy. Do they never rest? David is wonderful, setting aside an hour every evening before dinner, so we can chat – man to man. I tell him a complete pack of lies about how happy I am at Swallow House.

"Some great blokes," I tell him, "Henry has rather taken over from Geoff as my best chum", and we laugh as I regale him with tales of how at last I have left my prejudices behind, "I really like Brian, he's an absolute delight, queer as a coot, but a lovely man and I really like him."

"Dad you'll never change, you can't call anyone 'queer' anymore, he's gay and that's all. Still it's an advance for you Dad I must say. It's true what they say – you never stop learning eh?"

That's true, wisdom at last perhaps.

I listen to the tales of their great American adventure of schools and sport and amazing things I can hardly imagine. I feel a little jealous of Shanta's family who are so close to them all and see them frequently.

I fall asleep several times and wake to see them watching me, the children, Michael, muscular

140

and awkward, Tessa feminine and delicate with the most wonderful eyes and hair like her mum. Both are being unnaturally well behaved. They are doing their best to humour me. They genuinely care, but none the less I see them regarding me as a gentle old fossil that needs careful maintenance. I love them, how lucky am I? I have someone to love.

All too soon the third day comes and we head back to Swallow House, the mood has changed to quiet sadness. For me I am gratefulfor the break but deep down I want to get back to Henry and Brian and my room, where I can shut out the noise. I will be glad not to hear the children squabble, or Shanta playing nursemaid to me, who, despite all, she hardly knows. Underlying all these moods and reflections I am sad because I know that when they go back to America I may not see them ever again. David and Shanta pretend heroically that this is not the case. 'Nothing' is, for once, my friend.

141

After Shanta and David help me unpack, I shoo them out, give the kids a quick hug. I do not go down to see them off, I stay in my room and cry. I know the visit has enriched me, love has re-enlivened my reasons to live. I must keep these fires within me burning.

After the kids have gone and I have stopped my sudden aching sobbing, I enjoy being alone. Quiet in my room, silence overtakes me, I doze, I am tired, from the warmth of family. Johanna awakes and tells me not to be afraid, not to be fed up but to be the man she knew all those forty or so years ago.

They were great times, Johanna and I met two years after Margaret died. It was a chance meeting, she was a delegate at a conference I attended in Zurich. She really was a very attractive woman, and I was surprised when she spoke to me over coffee. I think she came my way to avoid the pack of hungry males, who, without exception, were attracted to this willowy blonde.

The rest as they say is history and we both went for each other like a couple of magnets. She was not only lovely to look at, she was just the most charming and engaging person to talk to. Over that coffee in the Intercontinental Hotel my life changed in the twinkling of an eye. From a lonely widower I became a hopelessly in love, bemused, and dazzled victim. It was wonderful, and it remained wonderful for the next thirty nine years.

The whirlwind romance lasted all that time, not once did I wake up without a smile on my face. Johanna became the epicentre of my life. When David was borne in 1968 our life was complete. We were getting on just a bit, so David was to be our only child. We both adored him and life was more or less perfect. One of the most wonderful thing about Johanna was her instinct about Margaret, she didn't avoid Margaret's memory, rather she helped me cultivate it and to cherish it. At the same time we lived life to the full, and David was and remained the light of her and my life.

David flew the coop when he was twenty seven and after that it was time that rushed by, his exciting life, the marriage to Shanta, the grandkids. How wonderful life could be.

It was Easter time in 2005, Johanna had gone to meet her old pals in Bristol. I was preparing the barbeque, Apple Tree Cottage was at its best at this time of year. The blossoms were breathtakingly beautiful. Johanna was late. Why hadn't she phoned? The hours passed, I paced the garden as the sun cooled, where ever could she be? It was nine o clock when a car drew up outside the house – at last I thought, but no, it wasn't her, it was a police car.

She had died instantly, as the single decker bus crashed head on, on a country route on her way home. I will never forget the drive to Bristol, silent and bleak in the back of the police car. I had told no one. There was part of me who did not believe that such a thing could happen. But, happen it did, there was my angel Johanna with just a small bruise on her face, quite still, and cold and dead. I am weeping again, how could this happen. I have never been so cold or so lonely. I shiver now, I cannot stop seeing through closed eyes.

This is worse than nothing, I must pull myself together. Here I am a spoiled old man, in the warmth of my comfortable room, protected from the rain that falls steadily through the autumn evening, but I am alive, I have people past and people present I love, and I have to move on. 'En theos', the 'god within', I will live and see them again.

I trudge down the corridor where I bump into Nigel.

"Fancy a game of golf tomorrow? Had a good game today, playing well." He looks away leaning on his frame. He's away with the fairies again.

I put my arm gently round his shoulder, "Cummon Nigel, we'll meet at ten if the weather's good." I find it hard to keep my balance and stagger a bit. "Bugger it Nigel, can't putt to save my life."

Nigel looks back at me. "What are you talking about John? Any way I must go to the shop."

"Come on Nigel, let's go back to your room." We walk slowly back down to the lockup. Nigel as docile as can be. How lucky I am. I wonder if I, am? In his gathering confusion Nigel seems content – does confusion or illusion have to be sad? Who knows?

Chapter 12

My career as a betting courier proved to be disappointing. Since my first assignments I was only met by Dave once. He was as jolly as ever, he introduced me to an associate who I did not like at all.

Once the fellowship I had perhaps promised myself with the charming Terry and Dave faded, my gambling career came to an abrupt end. Neither Terry nor Dave ever contacted me again.

Geoff spotted my lack of activity, and couldn't help but gently pull my wire.

"Not too busy then with your marketing consultancy, pity!"

"Oh bugger off Geoff. At least I had a go but I think the initiative came to nought."

"Not to worry, there's a rugby game on the tele on Saturday perhaps we can have a beer and watch the game."

There is a huge crash. Everyone is startled, I jump causing a shot of pain in my gammy leg, and some ladies gasp and utter little cultured screams. The carers start running toward the lounge door. Geoff bounds from his chair, I crane my neck to see what all the fuss is about.

Henry lies face down half way through the lounge doorway. A melee fusses round him, I am about the last to arrive on the edge of the wittering flock of alarmed residents.. A bell rings and the senior carer arrives at the run, we are all ushered away, there is blood plainly smudging the thick pink carpet.

"Back please, give us space to help Colonel Henry, please, please back off."

McCann arrives, and kneels beside Henry. After a second, she takes Alex to one side. She takes command. "Right, everyone, Henry has had a fall so please give us space to get Henry down to the medical wing. I would appreciate it if you all could go either to the conservatory or to your rooms. Thank you for your cooperation."

We all obey.

Eventually Henry is carted off to the medical wing. Henry is dead.

Geoff and I know instantly, I've seen dead people before. "Poor bugger's checked out."

"Look's like it." Geoff, looks around, several of the ladies are visibly upset.

"Not so much of the poor bugger, a pretty sharp and painless end I would say."

"You're not wrong Geoff, just wish we'd said good bye."

"Oh shit here comes Boyd, I don't think I can bear it Geoff, how about a snifter in my room."

"Good plan." We hurriedly scamper past Boyd, Geoff making a mumbled excuse.

Seated in the comfort of my rooms, I reach into the hiding pace for the single malt, McCann safely occupied with our late departed.

There's a knock on the door and Brian stands there pathetically tearful.

"Just heard, Henry's dead," at which point he shuddered, snivelling and being what I think is unstable. Geoff, as always, is much more sympathetic. He looks at me for assent.

"Come in, have a noggin it will make you feel better."

"I'm sorry," Brian snuffles.

"Don't be such a silly old queen, Henry went out like a light, what a lucky boy he was."

Brian smiles through his tears. "John darling, you've got such a way with words." We all laugh. We toast the lovely Colonel Henry and the bottle doesn't last very long.

"I wish I could go like that." Says Brian.

"Dear old Dan, would have loved to go like that." I retort.

"What about having a plan that we can all go when we feel we should?"

"Seems a bloody good idea if we could fix it." Is the whiskey talking? Or is it me?

"Why don't we get together all the boys? Then we could have a plan to help each other." Brian, now recovered from his grief, seemed enlivened by the debate.

"Good idea," said Geoff, "after all, we're all close to the exit, no point in making it more difficult for anyone, there's ethics and safeguards and all that, but I think we should start with some sort of consensus, We'll have to be careful about who and who does not know, McCann would have a fit."

"Old Henry was an example to us all." As soon as I said it I thought what a stupid remark that was.

"Anyway we're out of single malt. I need to go to the bathroom."

The assembly broke up Geoff and Brian leaving, Geoff still not wholly comfortable with dear Brian.

'Don't do anything silly'. It's Johanna, as I doze.

'Yes' echoes Margaret. 'You were always very impulsive.'

"I could be with you girls, what do think of that? A couple of pills and we can be together again."

'Not as simple as that' they come back in unison.

Hmphhh….. Would I? Could I? I slept like a top.

The next morning, I am not feeling well, but nevertheless I haul myself out of bed, do as Alex tells me and take my pills and eventually venture downstairs.

"Mr. Betts, may I have a word?" I recognise the lady as one of the more attractive of the female brigade. She is about my height, her face is handsome and she bares herself well. I try to gauge her age, 75 perhaps, but she remains very much a lady.

"Certainly Madame, what can I do for you?"

"May we take a coffee together?" She, says this rather demurely, she doesn't quite bat her eyes.

"Uuuhm, of course, where shall we sit?" What a useless fellow I am. In mild panic, I see Geoff watching, a bemused look on his face. I follow the spectre of my yearning youth, her legs are quite lovely. She beckons me to a seat in the conservatory.

"I'm Patricia, Patricia Hayes-Bowen."

"I'm John Betts."

"Yes, I know who you are, may I call you John? The reason I wanted to talk to you is.. Well, I heard you were starting a suicide club." She whispered the last few words.

I thought I'd misheard her, but nevertheless my heart nearly jumped out of my chest. "Madame…

"Patricia please."

"Patricia, I have no idea what you're talking about." I had to watch my language, I just can't believe that someone has betrayed our last night's conversation   already. Jesus it's been less than a day.

"Your secret is safe with me, John, it really is. There's so few of us who are compas mentis here, we have to stick together. Oh John, please don't be cross we're all in the same boat."

"It's that bloody 'fop' Brian, what in hell's name did he think he's doing, it was only a conversation for God's sake…….. Look I'm sorry Patricia, Mrs. Hayes…whatever

"Bowen, Hayes Bowen."

"Well Mrs, Patricia … sorry, but we were just getting ourselves together after dear old Henry,, fell over.. if you forgive the expression."

"Well John, if you'll forgive me for saying so, I think it's a jolly idea and we should certainly develop it." She looked out into the garden, "Let's face it John we're all here waiting for our exits, it seems sensible we should plan how we go, don't you think?"

Oh Bugger, what have I got myself into now? "Who else knows? Not that there's anything to know."

"Just me and Elizabeth Cummings."

She really is quite pretty, I am dying to ask how old she is but I dare not.

"Well let's both think about it shall we? I don't entirely believe that we'll feel the same when Henry's exit isn't so in our minds, as it were."

"Alright, may I seek you out again John?"

Suddenly I was lost for words. "Of course you can dear lady."

 I bowed a little and heaved myself from my chair desperately hoping that Patricia Hayes-Bowen found me attractive. Shame on me. Brian the old Queen has been yapping to all and sundry. I can't wait to get to him.

He sees me coming and darts into the lounge, bugger him I chase after him. Chasing implies speed of course and I guess I can rally to about two miles per hour. Brian takes refuge in the company of a gaggle of ladies. I join the group staring at Brian who obstinately avoids my gaze.

"Aren't things expensive in the shops." exclaims a lady who I think I recognise as the devout lady from the garden,

Another replies, "I shall go on a cruise, my last one was to Africa, South Africa, Harold and I enjoyed it so. I wonder if Harold will do it again?"

"Harold has been dead for fifteen years dear." Retorts another lady, she says it gently.

"Then perhaps we'll go to Australia, what do you think?"

The praying lady responds, "It depends on the costs you see, the shops are so expensive."

Brian is trying as hard as he can to pretend he is following all this confused claptrap. I tap him, none too gently, with my walking stick. I nod angrily, "My room, now!" I shape the words silently but with venom. I see Brian wince with something akin to fear.

In my room I wait, but I wonder what am I making this fuss about? Nothing? Is it nothing, a suicide club? There's a knock my door, its Brian accompanied by Geoff. I am taken completely off guard.

"Hello Geoff, come in Brian." "Drink anyone."

"Too early for me," says Geoff. Brian remains silent.

"Forgive my French but what the fuck did you think you were doing discussing our very private business with Lady Muck and co. for all I know. For Christ's sake it's a delicate and very private matter. What on earth were you thinking about? Brian, I'm sorry but you have to understand you're a bloody liability."

"Gosh did you know I've got the wrong socks on." Geoff lifts his trousers above ankle level.

"Oh for Fuck's sake Geoff don't be such a clod, Brian here has been and told everyone that we've formed a suicide/euthanasia club if Commandant McCann gets wind of it we'll be all confined to the lock up."

"Steady on Darling," Brian is wiping his fast receding hair line with one of his extravagant handkerchiefs. "I only mentioned it to Patricia, she's a lovely lady and I asked her to talk to you."

"Why did you mention it for God's sake its nobodys' business but ours."

Geoff who has taken umbrage by my attacking his 'socks' opener, "Yes steady John, don't fly off the handle."

I look at the floor, I wish Henry was here he'd know what to do.

"Are we abandoning our self-help project then?"

"Let's think about it some more." Opines Geoff professorially.

"Sorry Darling," says Brian, "but I'm sure we can trust Patricia."

I huff and they trudge out. My leg hurts.

Chapter 13

The palaver over our euthanasia idea seemed, like many things, to drift in and out of oblivion. Brian somehow has slunk back into my affections and nothing more has been mentioned. Geoff, socks still at odds, seems to be content, back, I assume, with his Particle Physics.

Nigel is rapidly deteriorating if not in body then certainly in mind. Despite his lamentable physical state he still rambles intermittently about golf. He makes a great song and dance about which course we are to play and reminisces interminably about his golfing prowess which I must assume was long ago.

"Tuesday, before the ladies, what do you think?" Here he goes again.

"Sorry Nigel the leg's not too good, have to pass I'm afraid."

"Pity, pity." Nigel turns and waddles on his Zimmer frame, muttering about how unreliable his golfing pals are. Poor man, soon for the lockup I would guess. But, to be fair Nigel, and for that matter a substantial number of other residents are regressing both physically and mentally. We hardly notice when one or other disappears into the lockup. I wonder if anyone would notice when it's my turn.

It is none other than Patricia Hayes-Bowen who gets the whole wretched conversation started again. I open my door to find the lady standing brazenly as if expecting to be invited in.

"Madame, to what do I owe this pleasure?"

"John, you don't mind me calling you John do you?"

"If you are pleased to do so, of course you may." I am embarrassed, ladies should not be in the gentlemen's corridor, this, is most unseemly.

"Shall we go downstairs, if you want to talk." I sound and feel cross.

I see her stiffen a little, she takes an audible breath, "Look John I'm not going to attack you or anything I just want us to carry on our discussion that's all."

I do not reply, simply put on my jacket and indicate that we must make our way downstairs. "Shall we take a walk in the garden, the weather seems pleasant?"

"As long as we can have our chat John, I know we shouldn't be overheard."

"Quite so." I feel very awkward, like a small boy walking into class with a girl he doesn't know whether he fancies her or not. My dignity is in tatters. Boyd waves an unmissable and mischievous greeting. I pretend not to see him. For some reason or another I am trying not to limp which is of course my default position. Why am I doing this? The consequence is that I lunge from side to side almost as if drunk. I am making a complete fool of myself. Damn this woman!

We are still walking in single file, she stops at the summerhouse a fairly dilapidated structure which like parts of Swallow House has a sort of faded glory. She sits, I find that the only place left, is to sit close to her. I stand my ground, am I being gentlemanly or afraid?

"And what is it you want to discuss?" I shuffle round my walking stick assuming anything but a stable posture,

"For goodness sake sit down John, and relax I'm not going to bite you."

I give in and slump beside her. She smells nice, not just her perfume but she smells like a delicate and wonderful female. My chin drops to the hand on my walking stick I am already defeated.

"Patricia, let me say at the outset, there have been no more discussions regarding the end of life issues we discussed the other night. I feel it was just a reaction really to dear old Henry popping his clogs so suddenly. I think we were all shocked, he looked so bloody well... I beg your pardon, but you know what I mean."

"John, don't take this the wrong way, but I would very much like to have a conversation about end of life, or tomorrow, or the circus, or chemistry as long as we could be friends."

I literally do not know where to look. I have no idea what to say, I don't even know if I want to say anything. I stare into the autumnal and skeletal rose garden, I am quite lost. Not 'nothing lost' but confused, complimented, even frightened by this lovely lady. I stand and begin to walk back to the house. I hear her say,

"John, we'll do this again shall we. Don't be afraid John, everybody needs somebody even at eighty four." She laughs lightly. "Or maybe eighty one."

I trudge back into the House, I am not only confused I'm exhausted. I need to have a nap. I ignore the grinning Bishop, and an assortment of nosey greetings. Everyone I am sure, is aware of my dalliance with Mrs. Hayes-Bowen. Their eyes penetrate even my back, I speed up as best I can, I have let myself down, I have left my girls down, this dreadful women has interfered with everything. My privacy, my relationship with Brian and Geoff, and now she's made a fool of me. I am relieved to be back in my rooms. I slump into the chair, my God what a morning it's been. As I bend to undo my shoes, there is a crash. I am on the floor, my shoulder hurts, there is blood in my mouth.

I don't have my bleeper to hand, it's another catastrophe, why am I so useless? I hear myself moan, I cannot move, as ever my gammy leg is somehow jammed under the chair. I think I'll have a nap.

I am thirsty, I open my eyes and the light is blinding.

"Hello, Mr Betts. How do you feel now? Can you hear me Mr Betts?" A sharper light pierces my eye, I stiffen, my shoulder stabs, where am I?

"Mr Betts, I'm doctor Ishan, you're in hospital and we think you've dislocated your shoulder."

What's he talking about? I fell out of my chair, bugger it, I was taking my shoes off .

"Drink" I croak.

A beaker is placed to my lips, the water is delicious, I didn't know water could be so good. I want more. A cool wind of blue, a smell of cleanliness, the image real or not is of a pretty nurse, she proffers the beaker again, as I reach forward my shoulder stabs me again. "Ooh! Hurts."

I am back, confined to some dreadful prison and again it is my own hapless fault. They all fuss round me, I notice I am trussed like a turkey at Christmas, my whole right side is bound and slung. No arm, no leg to speak of, what a shambles, just an old man who's crashing about causing mayhem, what a waste of space I am. Bugger, Bugger, Bugger!

All I want to do is go back to sleep. I dream of my girls again, they are both sympathetic and laugh about me falling over.

"Sober too," mocks Margaret.

"Back from an assignation," mocks Johanna.

Nothing takes over, I sleep and sleep and sleep. I wake, it is dark. Surely I would be less of a nuisance if I was dead. I wonder if Geoff has done his work on the 'the peaceful pill'? I drift sleepily and feel the chill of the lonely blackness. Every now and again I feel pain in my shoulder, in my arm. There are people, there is light. I am astonishingly thirsty, I might die of thirst – will anyone help? Let me go I want to go.

Margaret calls but from a huge distance, Johanna speaks but I cannot hear her, please let me go to the big sleep. It has to be better than this. Please give me something to slake my awful thirst. Is this the way we go gasping for the merest drop of water being strangled and choked with this arid pain? Let me go.

There is a soft wet sweetness on my lips. I thrust my tongue but it is welded to my mouth, but I so much want to drink. There is blinding light, I can hear someone, he is green and he or she is blue.

"Mr. Betts, Mr. Betts, can you hear me?"

Yes I can hear you, but that light bores into my eyes like a physical arrow it hurts, I close my eyes.

"Mr. Betts, Mr Betts can you stay with us?
Hello Mr. Betts, you're in the medical wing. Mr
Betts…. come on ."

'Oh why don't you fuck off! I want a drink,' I
open my eyes to the searing light, I try to move
my arms to signal for more water. Everything
hurts why can't they understand? At last there's
a cool hand on my neck and a beaker is put to
my lips, I am alive and it is true, water is life. A
cool flannel soothes my brow, my eyes slowly
acclimatise to the light. The green person is not
green at all he's a medic of some sort and the
blue person is the nurse I've seen before.
Confusion rains, there is no past no present just
the light. I am afraid, not of my discomfort but
of the vacuity of my mind. 'Come on Betts you
old fart get a grip.'

My life is wasting away, I don't want to live any
more. I know I want my life to come to an end
when McCann appears all sweetness and light.

She wakes me up, her smarmy voice pierces my rest, I hear her muttering to the duty nurse.

"How is he?"

"He's stable, we think he'll come out of it fairly well, the shoulder isn't badly dislocated, but at his age we'll have to see."

'At my age! If you please, when is the end the end? Sooner the better. I decide to keep my eyes shut and hope that McCann will retreat. No such luck she hovers over my like some perfumed vampire. I open my eyes.

"Oh John, so nice to see you recovering from your fall, you'll soon be up and about again," she looks up at the nurse for support. The nurse coos a reply which I don't get.

"Thank you Joan," I whisper back, I just want her to go away.

"I've been on the phone to David, I've told him you are well on the way to being up and about again but he's insisted on coming to see you, he should be here tomorrow."

Fuck this woman, if there is anything in this world I do not want to be it's a bloody burden on my son. What can I do, die that's what and I can put an end to all this nonsense. What do I do. I cry, the tears roll down my face.

"Ooh, don't cry John," McCann wipes away my tears. I can smell her perfume, I wish she'd just go away. I want a bottle, the last thing I want to happen is that I piss myself when McCann is attending me. I am lost, I do not know what to do. I am back at school and I do not want to wet the bed. The warm urine soaks between my legs I wince, does she know what's happening? Her eyes give her away, the unmistakable smell of piss overtakes her exuberant perfume, she winces ever so subtly. Despite her calling, old men pissing in bed are not her 'thing'. She straightens and leaves the room. I am relieved in more ways than one.

Chapter 14

Days have passed, I am, at last, sitting in a chair near my bed, Geoff and Brian have been to see me this morning which cheered me up a bit. I've been left in an awful quandary since David is rushing to my bedside. Of course I will be happy to see him but I am cross and remain so, that yet again, David has dashed across the Atlantic to see to his miserable and useless father.

David and Shanta arrive this morning, I have been prepared for their arrival, dolled up like a museum piece. A young man called Tomos has been introduced as my new carer. I objected, but I have little fight left in me. Tomos helps me dress and dashes back and forth to my rooms to get various shirts and jackets. Despite my lack of gusto there remains a bloody-mindedness which is vented on young Tomos. To his credit he does not blink but responds to my unreasonable requests with a meek but good humoured kindness.

Tomos' command of her Majesty's English is scant and this doesn't help, it would be amusing, except for my grim humour. He hails from Albania, he tells me and has been in this country for over five years. He is, he says, if I understand him correctly, a trained medic. I must confess I don't quite understand him but my decision is that he's a decent young fellow and we have to get on together. One thing is plain, he is generous and kind and strikes a lovely balance between subservience and genuine personal kindness. Despite all my miseries, Tomos is a positive gain.

"Your boy, he is fine man. He will be glad to see you in such good health with Tomos to be your friend."

"David is a fine man, as you say, and he will be glad about me getting care, but Tomos, I really don't want him upset in any way – do you understand?"

"Of course Mr. John, is OK if I call you Mr.John? OK?"

We've already been getting ready for over an hour and a half, David should be here any minute, I couldn't have done this alone, the thought comes crashing in, what a useless old bugger I have become. 'Calm down whispers Johanna, calm down, you're doing fine echoes Margaret.'

There is a tap at the door and David and Shanta dash across to me and hug me with a tender reserve, usually expressed when holding valuable but frail antique china. They are closely followed by McCann.

"Tomos, you may go." McCann, crisply orders Tomos.

"No stay, Tomos," I countermand, looking at McCann. I enjoy this tiny triumph. "I'd like

Tomos to meet David and Shanta, Tomos this is my son David and his wife my daughter in law Shanta." David and Shanta shake him by the hand and young Tomos seems embarrassed.

McCann then launches into a detailed explanation of Tomos's duties and my care plan. It is all excruciating, they're talking about me, an old fossil and how I/it can be preserved. McCann whispers when it comes to the costs of all this care. David nods, cost is not a problem. McCann leaves, as always I am relieved when she leaves the room, the waft of her perfume leaves like a vapour trail behind her.

There are symbols of my infirmity, a wheeled Zimmer contraption which is the most ghastly thing – ever. It shows the world that I can no longer propel myself around without this navy blue trike with the swallow house logo. My propensity for foul language is curtailed by the gracious presence of my lovely daughter in law. However I find it hard not to wince with the shots of pain that run like electrical shocks through my shoulder. Old age I reflect is not for sissies.

She looks so beautiful, her golden complexion, her fabulous shining black hair and her wonderfully graceful figure. As always, I am transfixed by her beauty. There is an absolute joy about seeing them together, I struggle to hold back my tears of affection. I don't think I ever really appreciated how much I love these two and the kids. They are all I ever wanted and wanted to be. I am at once immensely proud and happy of them and for them. They are the product of my life, they are the promise of things to come.

For the first time in many days we troupe to the guest dining room, Tomos trots behind keeping a keen eye on my Zimmer driving which is less than competent.

At lunch Tomos discreetly leaves, and David, Shanta and I have the most wonderful time. At least I do. There is an air that another crisis has passed and that I shall be fine and well again. In my heart I have my doubts but here we are perhaps in our final farewell. Time passes all too quickly and it's time for my loving kids to leave. This time I cannot contain my tears. Shanta envelopes me in a gentle warm hug, I try very hard to pull myself together. As if by some mystic call, Tomos appears. He stands and I see the tears in his eyes, what about his home? What about letting these youngsters go?

I snivel some more, David hides his regret, he smiles, breaks gently from me and they are gone.

"Come on Mr. John, let's get you back to your rooms." Gently, Tomos takes my arm and we make our way back to my lonely rooms, perhaps I can find a scotch, I don't know how many days have passed since I fell. Life goes painfully on.

My first reaction back in my rooms is to be alone, but Tomos, lurks he's doing something, I don't know what. We are ignoring each other, at least I am doing my best ignoring him. Why doesn't he go away? I want to be left alone to be sorry for myself.

"Mister John," I ignore him. "Mister John."

"Yes what is it?" I turn, why doesn't he bugger off?

"It is only three o clock, but maybe today?"

God bless Tomos, he is holding a glass of scotch, "Mister John, maybe today, to give you comfort, Is O.K.?"

From that moment on, Tomos and I get on like a house on fire. He sees me every morning when I get up, he helps me to go to bed at nine thirty every night, he answers my buzzer except on his day off. The costs of Tomos's administrations is probably very high like everything else in Swallow House. From the outset, Tomos is worth it. Things like putting on and taking off my shoes, helping me get dressed are an absolute Godsend, I hate to admit it but Tomos really is worth his weight in gold. He is Albanian, and I have no idea how he comes to be living here in England. We have innumerable chats about his homeland and how his father lost the family fortune to some corrupt Government minister. In fact Tomos seems to have an entirely ambivalent view of his home country, it is apparently both beautiful and bent. He has a sister who is in America. He is usually very cheerful but on occasions he can be melancholy.

My shoulder and all the associated parts like my ribs and shoulder blade are all very uncomfortable. I visit the lock up twice a week for physio therapy which for the most part I enjoy very much, especially when Ruth is in charge, she's really pretty and knows what's up. She cheers me up no end.

Life is slow, I sleep a lot. My afternoon naps seems to stretch into hours. My gammy leg usually wakes me up and if it's not my leg then it's my shoulder. Aches and pains are everywhere. David rings on the TV computer thing twice a week, I do wish he wouldn't, I find the conversations difficult, I have nothing to say.

Tomos has been deputed to teach me how to use a computer so that I can talk to David, Shanta and the kids and see them all. It is, I must say, magic at least the first few goes are, but then the awkward silences and the stuttered farewells begin to grate.

I am no longer allowed out on my own. I now have a wrist band that sets off an alarm if I move outside Swallow House. If I am escorted by Tomos, he fiddles with the door mechanism and we're allowed to leave the eagle eye of McCann and co. Since my accident I have only left the home once, with Tomos, to have a scan on my shoulder which is apparently now totally healed though you could have fooled me.

My language, which has never been correct, has sunk to new lows with every other word the 'F' word. It's 'F' this and 'F' that. Tomos responds in type when we are alone and we sometimes count who can use the 'F' word most in a given time. I usually win. When we are out in polite circles, with Geoff or Boyd, then I enjoy watching them wince as the 'F' word tumbles out. If there are ladies present, then as ever, I seem to be able to behave, much to all their relief.

Tomos has made such a difference, particularly in the mornings when I get up, he is most helpful and despite my curses he gently cajoles me into the bathroom, the shower, helps me rub down and to dress, best of all he helps me with my shoes and socks, you cannot imagine what a difference this makes. He does all this gently and humbly never intruding on my privacy. In a matter of days he has become indispensable.

Each day when Tomos leaves me I feel a certain weightlessness. I fight not to stay in my rooms, it's so easy to shut the door and doze the day away. Down stairs, apart from dodging Boyd, it is not easy to shut your eyes and blot out the desiccating stink of decaying old age. I am part of it I know, but I have to keep fighting.

Swallow House has a diary of events to entertain the inmates. Mostly this entertainment consists of third rate entertainers who are hybrids between children's clowns and out of tune musicians. Occasionally the local children's choir appears and they are very good, driven as they are by their choir master who looks about fifteen.

We do have a nice piano, and one or two of my fellow inmates play it now and again. One of HB's pals plays extremely well and sometimes gives little concert performances of a classical nature. I love these, but sometimes she sits down without so much as a warning and I miss her little but beautiful interludes. My language when this happens dives into the obscene. Johanna you see played the piano, I just love it when whatshername plays, I close my eyes and

hear my lovely Johanna play and speak above,
but with the melodies. The sweetest
Scandinavian nuances, the notes so gentle and so
salving. Yes, the piano interludes are the best.

Chapter 15

There is excitement afoot, HB's chum, the one who plays the piano is to be visited by her niece who is apparently an accomplished piano player like her aunt. She has consented to give a concert this afternoon. Despite my ever present aches and pains, Tomos and I are doing our best to dress me up for this splendid occasion. My shoulder and arm remain awkward, my left arm hangs now that I'm out of my sling. Bloody deformed, even more than before. Nevertheless, for the first time in ages, I feel positively excited.

HB it must be said has kept her distance since the arrival of Tomos, and I am not sure if I'm pleased or disappointed. In any event I find myself sitting next to her. Whatshername with the big boobs introduces her niece who is disappointingly unglamorous. She's middle aged (whatever that means) and makes McCann look positively Hollywood.

When she starts to play it is another story. The music is sublime, she is, at least to my ear, terrific. The end comes all too soon and the thirty or so residents clap with surprising enthusiasm. Maybe they're not so idiotic after all.

"Wasn't that wonderful?" Patricia Hayes Bowen aka HB has her hand on mine, at first I am shocked then the coolness of her touch invades my senses. The electricity and the coolness combine to almost paralyse my mind. In rush a myriad of sentiments, of belonging, of memories, of ecstasy all in one. Peace perhaps, all anger is washed away, indeed her simple and light touch bathes me in a delicious light. I am instantly in confusion.

"Yes, it was, and so are you HB."

"Am I still no more than a soft pencil?" Her eyes laugh at me.

I cannot remember HB's name. Bugger! What do I say next? I know,

"You'll have to put up with HB from now on, I won't change, HB is lovely – I'm sorry if it upsets you." Then it comes to me, 'Patricia', not Pat. I think I prefer HB.

She removes her hand, it's as if the light has gone out. She looks at me, smiles, "I suppose HB will do, but not in company please, John."

The afternoon tea is splendid with HB, the pianist, whatshername and the dreaded McCann. The music has lifted us all, even McCann is all sweetness and light.

I was relieved that the dreaded Boyd was not part of the VIP table after the concert. This must have pissed the Bishop off greatly. It gives me a malevolent and secret joy. When Boyd, sidles up, I feel rather smug, one up on the silly old bugger. He doesn't ease my contempt when he praises the concert, I instantly dismiss his

186

comments, as I do to his cricket codswallop. However I have to admit that his knowledge of music is not bullshit, he really knows what he's talking about. In fact he clearly knows more than me. And then he says,

"When I was in the army," you could have knocked me down with a feather.

"You were in the army Boyd?"

"Oh yes, I was in the Chaplain's Department, served in Ireland twice with two different outfits."

"Well bless my soul, never knew that Bishop." Shall I tell him about the shortest army career of all time? Can't help it, it all comes out and we chat for the next hour. Bugger it! Bishop Boyd is not such a sanctimonious prick any more.

In my room I doze, it's been a good day except for the continuous discomfort and pain from my leg and shoulder. Tomos has dispensed my pain killers, he seems to know when I need them as opposed to a glass of scotch. The pain is just that, a pain, but it slows me down. I know that if I sleep too much, slow down too much, I will begin to die. The elephant is always in the room. Do I want to carry on with all this bother, pain, the agony of each new day, the unwinding out of bed, the struggles to get dressed? It's all a tremendous fag, an effort and I am beginning to see why some people want to pack it all up.

Nothing, that's the bloody killer. Sleeping, waking, hurting, struggling, crapping and trying to sleep, all for nothing. I sleep.

Tomorrow is here already, I wake before the alarm, the window curtains leek a slow grey light, I turn and extricate myself from my warm bed and stagger to the loo. I sit and take stock of my physique. Shoulder, better? Too early, to say but my gammy leg as always is just the same. I listen to my heart beat, it thumps regularly, I dump my troubles and prepare for another day.

"Don't be so miserable," scolds Margaret. "I think you should start making up with HB." She laughs, almost a nervous giggle.

"Margaret is right, you should have some fun, may be HB will cheer you up. Remember how I cheered you up? A bit of Scandinavian massage. You used to like that. A bit strenuous now I suppose." They both laugh in unison.

There's a tap on the door and in comes Tomos. "Good morning Mr John, I hope you slept well."

And so another day starts. I breakfast with my new chum Boyd, I even close my eyes for grace. Geoff, no mention of his socks, is serious, reading his Guardian newspaper, and grunting in and out of our conversation. I think perhaps he's miffed because Boyd and I are now chums – ex-army chaps, both! Nigel is absent committed I learn to the lockup, can't say I'm surprised. Brian sidles in late sporting an outrageous and outdated cravat. We are now the senior men in the House, average age around 84 ++ though I have no real idea.

Geoff folds his paper, "Gentlemen, I have some news." He's so professorial, we all turn as one. "This is strictly confidential." Brian fiddles with his hearing aid. We are all ears, what's up? I am languidly interested, it is better than nothing, that's for sure. "Can you all make a private meeting tonight before dinner at say six, my room?" There's a pregnant pause, "I've got news from the end of life people. Bishop after our conversation you are of course excused if you please, but I ask you keep our confidence."

"I shall think about it," Boyd sweeps his face with his napkin, "In confidence of course." With that he gets up and leaves.

Geoff puts his fingers to his lips, "Strictly confidential." He too gets up and leaves.

Later, at the appointed hour, there are six of us assembled in Geoff's room, Myself, Brian,

Geoff, Boyd, HB and she of the big bosom. We turn up on time with everyone hushed as if some great accident was about to befall us. There is a collective quiet, a solemn expectation.

I look round and I am immediately aggravated to see that HB is sitting next to Geoff, she is very close to him physically, her side touches him. I feel my blood begin to boil. I am shown to Geoff's armchair, I assume, because of my hopeless infirmities. If HB fancies Geoff, then this meeting will really have meaning for me. I shall be off!

Geoff brings us to order, suddenly he has changed. He is now the Professor, he is going to teach us, he is going to be 'the man', I notice HB cocks an ear, she's in awe of Geoff and possibly his silly odd socks. I twitch in my chair.

"We are here," announces the Professor, "to discuss a matter of great sensitivity, and although we are a group, of great personal privacy. We will be discussing end of life

191

protocols, themselves considered to be outside the law. Further I will be sharing with you data I have in my possession, which in law, I should not." He pauses and looks at each of us in turn, as if to make sure his message has sunk in. "I want, therefore, your assurance that each of you in turn swear to keep all the matters we discuss as absolutely confidential."

"Mrs. Hayes-Bowen, may I have your solemn assurance?"

"You have my assurance." Replied HB, her voice firm and magically musical.

And so on round the room. I nod and mumble my assent.

There is a knock on the door , it is Alex, "Wondered where everyone is," he said chirpily, "Supper in twenty minutes," With that. he exits and is gone.

"Bloody Commandant's spy, can't go to the loo without that bitch interfering." I immediately knew I'd overdone it.

"John, there is no need to be so coarse." HB scolds me. I am mortified and humiliated. I think I blush – surely not!

It's Boyd who speaks up for me, "Well he has a point, may I suggest that I let it be known that we have a prayer group that I will convene from time to time."

Geoff, ever the Professor, "Will that be acceptable do you all think?"

"What if other people want to join?" asks She of the big bosom.

"Leave that to me," answers Boyd, I can't help but admire his sudden and decisive intervention, it is as if Boyd is one of my brother Officers.

The meeting is brought back to order. "This merely illustrates how careful we have to be." Geoff the Professor is firmly back in charge. He continues round the room seeking his 'solemn assurances.'

The rest of the session is about a book which Geoff has acquired, it's about sticking our heads into plastic bags, getting paralytic and taking lots of pills, I find it hard to follow and I am instead transfixed on HB's hands. If she touches Geoff he won't need a pill, I'll kill him and that's a fact.

The meeting ends, and just like meetings I used to chair all those years ago, the date for the next meeting is fixed. We are all again sworn to secrecy and Boyd insists on closing the meeting with a prayer for heavenly guidance. For once I bow my head. What a good bloke Boyd is.

Chapter 16

I am not in the least concerned about being a
member of the 'Do it yourself suicide club', I
left the meeting last night, cross with HB, and
cross with myself for not doing anything.
Tomos knew straight away that something was
wrong but I kept it and will keep it to myself.

The girls know somethings up, they scold me,
and laugh together about my crass ineptitude. In
bed this morning after a sleepless night I could
only get patchy chats with Johanna and
Margaret. They were, for once, no help at all,
just taking the piss out of me for being "a silly
boy", whatever that means.

Because I didn't sleep I feel lousy, Tomos helps
me dress, but I am absolutely tired at the start of
the day. I look in the mirror and see what an old
wreck I am.

"Mr John, you are not good today, maybe you
go back to bed ..," He witters on, about me

sitting down and even he annoys me. Why is HB such a bitch?

"Mr John. What is problem, you not good, please I think you go back to bed I fetch lady for you from medical centre."

"Tomos, help me with my shoes and for Christ's sake shut up… I'm fine just had a bad night that's all, now pass me my shoes."

He responds but I can see he is nervous, he fusses over me. I wish he would bugger off. It's all HB's fault, why did she ignore me? What have I done, nothing that's what, I've done nothing. Maybe she wants Geoff to be her new pal, I don't care, but I know I do care and it makes me feel unwell. I think I will go back to bed.

I can't sleep. Tomos slinks off, and sure enough the nurse appears, quickly followed by the dreaded McCann. I wish they'd all go away, all I need is sleep, though I have a headache, and my balance is no good. Maybe I'll send for Geoff and his funny pill or plastic bag or whatever. My blood pressure is high or low or something, but they won't get me in the lock-up, no bloody way. Wait till I see Tomos, I'll give him what for, all I want is to be left alone to rest.

Time hangs heavily, dead birds tweet no more, I can't even play with myself I'm too old and useless. It used to be a way of making me go to sleep, but I can't even do that anymore.

"John, Mr Betts", it's that awful McCann, "may we come in?"

She doesn't wait for an answer, behind her is that Indian fella, the doctor.

"Good morning Mr. Betts I was on site so I'd just like to check if all's well. May I?"

Usual stuff, listens to my chest checks my blood pressure again, I wish he'd bugger off, all I need is rest.

"All seems to be fine Mr Betts, all you need is a little rest."

I grunt, as if I didn't know. Now go away all of you I just want to sleep.

Sleep eventually intervenes, Margaret and Johanna are quiet, HB appears in my dream, but horror of horrors she's on Geoff's arm and they are eating fish and chips from odd coloured socks. I wake with a start. Tomos is standing over me.

"You OK, Mr. John?"

"Yes, I'm fine. Tomos. Stop fussing."

"Visitors, Mr. John, I bring them in, no?"

Before I can adjust or even sit up, in walk Geoff and HB. I cannot believe my eyes, the bastard Geoff is making it with HB! I am lost for words.

"How are you young man? We heard you weren't well so we've just come in to see if you're up to speed."

"How are you John?" HB asks.

What is up? Why is she with Geoff? I find it hard to speak, I am beside myself with rage. How dare they come in here, that son of a bitch with his odd socks, and HB who looks so lovely. I can't help looking at her dress, has Geoff been interfering with her? Does she like him? Does she know how much I like her? Confusion floods in, I am drowning in adolescent jealousy. I know it, but I can't do anything about it.

"Go away!" I snap and instantly regret it. They are beating a confused retreat, but just as they make to leave I blurt,

"Sorry just waking up, very kind of you." I gabble my words, I sound as if I'm demented. I think I am demented. "Just woken up, you see, didn't expect guests, please forgive me."

They both turn HB bumping into Geoff who in his confusion almost embraces her. A sharp pain runs through me, all of me. Am I seeing what I think I'm seeing, Geoff, 'Professor odd socks' making away with my girl? They separate and Geoff sits on the bed and HB sits in the chair on the other side of me. As I look between them the rainbow of pain stays, its tight from my stomach to the back of my eyes, I don't know what to do, or what to say.

Geoff whispers, "We are afraid that perhaps last night's meeting may have spooked you, if so I'm very sorry."

HB pipes in, her voice low and rather sensual, "Dear John, we both hope that you are not in any way upset about what we talked about."

What a lot of nonsense, I couldn't care less about the plastic bag or the bloody pills and gin,

"Not at all," I smile as if all is well. I feel my smile freeze. 'Oh HB if only you knew?', but of course she doesn't and she's a number with the Professor, the bile rises again.

As if to show how unconcerned I am, I announce my immediate plan to get out of bed and come down for tea. They look at each other as if I am somehow deranged. HB speaks first, she takes my hand,

 "Please John, take your time none of us are without a little tired spell now and again."

"No, no, I'm fine," I protest, I want to keep an eye on Professor Odd-socks and his philandering. "No I'm keen to get up, have a cup of tea, please humour me, I'll come down and we can have a cuppa."

Days follow, and I find myself being tongue tied whenever I meet HB, I keep my eyes open but I don't see her and Odd-socks together, they must be hiding their affair. I stumble about, I really am tired but I have to pretend I am well to Tomos, who watches me like a hawk. His friendly banter grates sometimes but he remains indispensable when it comes to getting me up, and for that matter going to bed.

Johanna and Margaret are very quiet, they hardly speak to me at all. I miss them as my minutes and hours are spent watching HB even from a discreet or often absurd hiding places, behind the newspapers, via reflections. My friend Boyd, has noticed something is up, so my frantic shadowing of HB becomes even more ridiculous. I am at once aware of my silly behaviour but at the same time unable to stop it.

Pretending to be not tired when in fact I feel exhausted is not easy. My obsession with following HB around is not lessening, so each day I drive on although I am out on my feet. I pretend to Tomos, to everyone, that I am as fit as a flee but it is bloody hard. I slip up to my room, hopefully unnoticed most afternoons and grab a snooze. I am afraid I might sleep too long and be discovered, I am in constant stress about HB and my fitness, and my jealousy being discovered.

Chapter 17

Boyd whispers that we are to have another 'prayer meeting' apparently 'Oddsocks' has some news on ways of doing away with ourselves. I am so miserable I can't think of anything more appropriate. The meeting is to be held in Boyd's quarters and is strictly by invitation only.

It's the same crew, Boyd, Geoff aka Oddsocks, Brian, HB, me and Vanessa Wainright of the enormous bosom. Boyd starts with a prayer for guidance, a lot of baloney if you ask me, but I bow my head with one eye fixed on HB who is sitting primly on her own to my right. She sees me eyeing her, I immediately look away and feign a grunt as if my leg was being particularly painful.

We are then treated to another lecture about confidentiality from the Professor who is getting on my nerves. I sit there fuming, HB is transfixed by his blather. He eventually gets round to his notes from a book that he has acquired from those who run the world's leading DIY suicide group.

Everyone seems to hang on his every word, and we all engage in a ridiculous debate about assisted and non-assisted methods of doing ourselves in.

Then comes the shocker, that Professor Geoff, 'Oddsocks' himself is in the process of acquiring a lethal but apparently peaceful pill that we can buy into for around a couple of hundred pounds a head.

The debate then gets a little heated about forming a sub-committee, about allowing anyone to be allowed to take the pill. An argument about living wills, other claptrap about confidentiality, and who should be in charge of what. We are brought to an abrupt halt by the statuesque Ms. Wainwright, whose voice is stronger than I ever imagined.

"Who, among us here wants to end their life now?" She looks around the room like a bird perched on her own chest. There is a crashing silence.

I hear myself, "I'm eighty five next week and I think I'm ready to go." I can't believe I've said that. There is a shocked silence. I continue to ramble, my mind is in a complete muddle. 'My leg hurts, I have arthritis everywhere, my David dashes over the Atlantic if I should so much as sneeze, I am in short a miserable old man and a nuisance to boot." I feel as if I want to cry but I dare not. The silence continues.

Eventually it's Brian who pipes up, none too convincingly as far as I am concerned. "Darling, we all absolutely love you, I so much enjoy our little drinkies, our little chats, you can't mean it darling, I should miss you dreadfully." He tucks his huge silk kerchief into his pocket after blowing his nose, I think he is about to cry as well.

205

Boyd hurrumps! "Look dear boy I don't think this is a proper forum for this sort of conversation. It brings us, I fear, to the very nub of the argument." He pauses.

Suddenly HB is in her feet and she just edges up to me, takes my hand in hers and says, "You are without doubt the silliest man I've ever met, but also one of the most lovely, I don't want you to say another word, except to invite me out for lunch tomorrow." She looks down at me with her lovely blue eyes, her perfume is so lovely it's painful, her hand on mine is like a silky feather, her breath is sweet as any flower. I am lost. "If you weren't so pathologically shy I'd have asked you before, I tried but you ran away." She looks up and sees she has everyone's rapt attention. Then she kisses the top of my forehead, and I start to cry.

Everyone stands and shuffle embarrassed by my childish rant. Only HB stays put, offers her hand and I stagger to my feet. 'Oddsocks' and

Boyd pretend to be in deep consultation, Brian continues to weep silently, and Wainwright rising to her full and curious gait stands towering over HB. "We should have some music nights sharing our favourite disks or some piano stuff, I think I'd enjoy that." How kind is she?

We are called to order and 'Oddsocks' who tells us once more the necessity for complete secrecy. He still wants his two hundred pounds from everyone and tells us what to do. We disburse, my thoughts of suicide dissolved into excitement and anticipation of tomorrow's lunch.

Brian and Wainwright follow me closely, I am at once embarrassed and overwhelmed by the spontaneous love everyone has shown me. I am warmed and confused in equal measure. I am a frustrated old bean with a zest for life yet, trying to escape the curmudgeonly old fart that I have become.

Wainwright stops at my door, puts her arm round me and smiles, "More music, that's what you want, John, but not on your own. Let's get together, a few of us and have a nice evening, shall we?"

For the first time for many days I look up I see her kind face, she is lean with clear blue eyes, she has enormous bags under her eyes but despite that she smiles with those lovely blue eyes. Her hair is silver and precise, her jewellery is neat and understated, she is both kind carer and sister figure all at once. I cannot find the words to say 'thank you'. I fumble with my door key, Brian takes them from me opens my door and shuffles in beside me. When the door closes, he hugs me so tightly.

He lets me go after what seems an eternity, "Shall we have a little drinky darling, and cheer ourselves up a bit?"

I nod, and as I reach for my hidden bottle of single malt, "Why not, bloody good idea, and Brian thank you, you are a lovely pal."

Before he hugs me again I bring out the bottle and glasses, like a shield to ward of the gay spirits. As I hand him his glass, I know I really love this guy like a brother. It dawns on me for the first time in many, many months that here in Swallow House I do have a family. There are times to be enjoyed, every moment has value.

"Cheers Brian."

Chapter 18   'HB'

My second husband Lionel was a complete
bastard, I don't like to be vulgar but I cannot
think of another word that suits. He didn't
knock me about physically except during our
sexual encounters but he constantly brow beat
me, in a never ending battle which could only
and always did, result in a victory for him. Sir
Lionel Bowen, as he became, was apart from
being a bully, very charming and outwardly
kind. No one had any idea about how miserable
it was to live with him. His constant preening,
and his condescending sharp wit wore me down,
till eventually he died and I must say I was
greatly relieved after twenty one years of
outward peace but inner turmoil. Few people
admit it, but the fact is at sixty four, I at last, laid
down my battered shield and for the first time in
twenty one years could relax.

Lionel being the swine he was, left all his estate
to his beastly daughters, Marie and Penelope.

Both, suddenly and conveniently, assumed I had independent means and sold the house from under me, and I stumbled on for another twenty years, I don't know quite how, except for Timothy's compensation and widows' pension package which had lain untouched for twenty years or more

I am lucky I can afford Swallow House, and here I am, actually quite happy. Eighty plus years old and secure at last.

The one thing I have done well, is look after myself. I don't want to sound vain but I have and still do look after myself. I may be eighty odd but I don't think I look it. Life hasn't been that easy, my darling son Bernie, Bernard Timothy Hayes actually, was born as a Downs child, we loved him to bits and we were heartbroken when he died from congenital heart failure when he was less than ten years old. That was hard, no one knows how much we loved Bernie. I smell his sweetness still, I feel

211

his gossamer hair as light as a butterfly wing, and I still feast on those big brown eyes that adored me, and his huge sweet smile that said thankyou everyday It was almost as if he's never left my womb. We were so close. Every day I held him and caressed him, he always loved me back and his Dad too. One of the most wondrous moments of my life was when the doctor told us that little Bernard was not perfect, he would be sickly and he was Downs syndrome. Tim, Bernie and I hugged with such love as it was almost impossible to bear.

As time passed we saw Bernie fail, his heart waring out from the age of nine. We tried so hard to keep him with us, to hold on to him, but he slipped away one winter evening when my lovely Tim, was away working in Canada. I have never been so lonely.

It could have been worse were it not for a young lady doctor, a trainee paediatrician who was working at my local surgery. As Bernie

struggled I became frantic and rang everyone I
could think of for help. It all seemed so useless,
I helped my darling little Bernie as he struggled
to breathe and no one came – no ambulance, no
doctor, - it seemed as if the world had
abandoned us, little Bernie most of all. I
screamed with frustration. I hardly heard the
doorbell. With Bernie in my arms, he was quite
a heavy child I staggered to the door where Dr.
Dotty Knight, stood, she looked like a school
girl.

"Yes, what do you want?" I was angry, but
before I could even let her answer she was
already half holding little Bernie,

"Dr. Knight, Dotty," she said, "let's get the little
one comfortable shall we?"

There was something about her, maybe the relief
of support, but she swept in, holding her bag
with one arm supporting Bernie. I let her lead,
nodding toward the lounge where we laid Bernie

down, all my fight and resolution gone, as Dr Dotty, did all she could for my lovely Bernie.

Despite her ministrations my little lovely boy stopped breathing, and slipped away, his sweet head slack against the pillow where he now lay. Dr, Dotty held me in her arms and we wept together, me and this stranger, this slip of a girl. Then the paramedics arrived to be taken aside by the young doctor.

Then was the most desolate silence I have ever experienced. Dr.Dotty took charge she wrapped Bernie so neatly and sweetly in soft white sheets. She offered me my son. I kissed him, and Dotty took him and gave him to the paramedic lady, who with enormous tenderness, took my hand and let me kiss again, this time him goodbye for ever.

Tim arrived the following day. He looked as if he had aged a hundred years. We held each other and sobbed till tears came no more. Dotty Knight called and did all she could to help, but despite her and many others there was no consolation. We just held on to each other.

To cremate or bury, what a desolate choice. Tim and I had each other but two torn hearts do not easily heal. It was harder than I imagined to lean on Tim, I think he felt the loneliness too.

We eventually started to live again in our empty world. Tim's firm were marvellous and he had a month off to help me but even then I knew that Tim worried about his work. He was the type of man who was as dependable as rock, he would never let anyone down. I saw him twitch and fidget as he answered phone calls about when he could get back to the job.

We had been married twelve years when Bernie died and the following year I lost my lovely Timothy to an accident. He'd been working in Canada, building a port or blowing up a mountain, I only vaguely understood or cared what he did. All I knew was he did whatever he did, well

When Tim was snatched away, I was hopelessly lost. I no longer had either of my beautiful boys, and life was a terrible void. I still feel that icy void sometimes, but I am calmer now, there is comfort in my age. A certain quiet, where there is no absolute loneliness, but sweet memories of little plump Bernie so trusting at my breast, his warmth and love permeate the years gone by. Timothy too, such a funny and warm partner who although he travelled a lot, never let a day pass without a phone call from where ever in the world he was. His beautiful voice almost touching me over the airwaves.

So being alone then, was like being dropped into a frigid dark sea of emptiness. I moped about quite deaf to my family, my mum and dad, my friends all of whom were married. I just went about in a daze.

About eighteen months after Tim had died I went to dinner, I was cajoled really by Amy Price, my neighbour. It was there I met Lionel

Bowen, he was all charm and good looks. I just went along with the flow and over the next year Lionel and I became really good friends. I really liked him, I was bewitched by his charm and wit. He made me laugh which was like a shining light and I began to live again. His daughters from his first marriage were just kids and I took their aloofness in my stride. I tried really hard to like them, to embrace them, but Penelope in particular was always a resentful child. Her mother had run away with the gardener or some such, I could hardly believe my luck. I never wondered why?

Lionel didn't rush to become my lover, he was as I said charming and kind. We had a small wedding and we honeymooned in Paris, I was swept away with the charm and romance. My first inkling of the real Lionel happened on our wedding night. It was only our third or fourth coupling, the others had been a little uncertain, not awkward but a little like adolescents. However in Paris that night Lionel began to

show his real colours. He became my first
experience of a really selfish boorish beast. The
thing that appalled me most was not the
indulgent sex, the things he insisted we tried,
things I found repulsive, it was that he seemed
absolutely unaware of my disgust and distress.
There we were, in one of Paris's most iconic
hotels and second Mrs Lionel Bowen was
buggered by this ghastly man. From that night
on, and there were many more to come, I lived
in fear and loathing of Lionel, and for twenty
years my opinion of him never changed.

I suppose I put up with Lionel despite all his
controlling in and out of bed, because we lived
well. I performed a bit like an old fashioned
courtesan, I co-hosted dinner parties, we
travelled widely, I even steered the two girls
through to their weddings. I got on better with
Marie than Penny who was always a spoilt bitch.
Their father doted on them, gave them
absolutely everything and showered money on
them when they married. When Penny was at

last married off I felt maybe Lionel and I could have a new beginning. It was not to be. Lionel by now was philandering like nobody's business, which I came to terms with. My menopause I fought largely in isolation, for which I am truly thankful.

Lionel didn't mind me shopping but every month he went through the bank statements with a tooth comb. I do believe that if Lionel had his way he would have rationed the toilet paper. Everything, what we ate, where I shopped, what holidays, when I serviced my car, Lionel dictated. We even fought over which hairdresser I should use. The girls on the other hand could do as they liked.

In public, though, Lionel was charming and considerate, all our friends thought 'how lucky' I was. Little did they know, that I wept before sleep most nights, that I held on to my sanity because of Timothy, that lovely gentle generous love, and of course my beautiful Bernie.

Through all this time Dr Dotty was a tower of strength, she had gone on to be a Paediatric Registrar at the Hospital and she got me to volunteer for the Downs Syndrome Association, which I loved and still love. Helping Mums in the DSA was always a wonderful lift for me, I threw myself into the work and saw my little Bernie in so many gorgeous kids. Many Downs children live a good deal longer than my own child and in some ways I pined for Bernie's older years that we'd lost for ever.

As Penny so cruelly put it, "Been working off your guilt again, Patricia?"

I used to bite my tongue, but I grew to dislike Penny nearly as much as I disliked her father.

Lionel was a big chunk of my life, I cannot but be ashamed of myself having thrown everything I had away. There was a before and after, before was wonderful, and after has been a little lonely, a few small adventures, but all in all, I have no complaints.

Chapter 19

Swallow House Community is a business that seems to catch all, it is a property business, the cottages, a retirement apartment complex the main House, and a nursing home. I came here on the advice of my solicitor Harry Bryan. Although Harry was an old friend of Lionel I quite liked him and he certainly liked me. I had rebutted his advances several times over the years, but Harry knew how to behave and always withdrew his not altogether unwanted advances with little embarrassment and good humour.

When Lionel died, which he did in bed with another woman, praise be! There was a great hullaballoo. However, Harry and I conspired to hide the unpleasant facts from his daughters, by then, both married.

The lady in question, who I understood had been trapped under Lionel's not inconsiderable frame for some time. Lionel had expired it seemed 'on the job', little did she know how lucky she was not to be face down. Harry, discreetly, paid her off. (legal fees?)

It was still a shock for me, when, I found out at the reading of Lionel's will that the house I lived in was in trust for his beastly daughters. All my equity of twenty years previous was not mentioned, I was at the mercy of Penny and Marie. Their father had still not let me go.

Harry to his everlasting credit had kept the compensation for dear Tim's death separate from the estate and so I was at last released from Lionel's controlling hand. He was dead and I admit, I was glad he was dead.

It was 1998 and I was 64 years old and free at last. My only link I cared about was the DSA and so I threw myself into the voluntary work as I could. There was a lot of humbug about me not being able to work because I had recently been bereaved. It made me furious, so I ignored all the caveats and did my bit with my lovely mums and dads, and their beautiful children.

It was at a charity conference in Bristol that I had my one and only sexual adventure since Lionel died. We were in a quite nice hotel and Dave, I think, was a volunteer from Leicester. I'd sat next to him that afternoon, he seemed a nice chap. He'd fathered a Downs baby who'd died at a very young age and he had broken up with his wife. My heart went out to him, and we had dinner and then more drinks, but he was such a kindred spirit. He appeared, albeit through a bit of an alcoholic haze, to have been considerably younger than me. At 65, I think I was rather complimented by his attention. In any event, there followed a sexual episode, that, compared with Lionel, was very gentle. For me, it was an odd adventure. It passed in a blur, noted only as my closing down performance. I'm not at all sure what Dave thought of it, but I missed him at breakfast and have not heard from him since. I can only assume that he was not that excited.

I lived alone for another fifteen years then after a the catastrophe of my house's drainage. The experience persuaded me that being a lone householder was a bad idea. I sold the house and moved here to an apartment in Swallow House Community. Over the years my friends have faded away most of them married, died or moved. Some widows like me have moved back to be with their kids. Many of the others have tried to make me meet other lonely men, believe me there are thousands, but after Tim, there is no one, no one, just Tim.

The only constant friend has been Dr Dotty who still comes round at least monthly and we go out for lunch and bit of girl talk. The one thing I do miss is that I am no longer involved in the Downs Syndrome Association. I think I was always a bit afraid that Dave might turn up one day at the Dorset Branch and I would have died with embarrassment. Dotty is now a Consultant Paediatrician and close to retirement herself, she is the only one who I told about Dave. Dr Dotty laughed and told me I should put myself about a bit more. It was a good gossip.

I can see why people get old once they move into retirement places. I'm not shy, no one would be after living with Lionel, but I did find it difficult to socialise. This is an odd place with a very mixed bag of all sorts. I sat in my little apartment tucked up for weeks. I only emerged for meals and then I didn't talk much. I just watched. Some were smart, some were scruffy, some were talkative, some were quiet, some, were clearly hovering between the retirement apartments and the nursing home. Some were self-aware and some quite lost.

Since Margaret McCann arrived, about a year after me things have really smartened up a lot. Everything is cleaner, the meals are better and McCann and her staff seem to be great organisers and housekeepers. I admire her, she's smart to look at and smart in her management, a really good example of a girl who's on top of her job. Alex, her henchman is a fine fellow who is just so reliable, he treats me like his aunt. I'm sure all the other ladies feel the same.

My closest friend in here is Elizabeth, Elizabeth Wainwright, she's my age and a very bright girl. Elizabeth is thin as a rake but she has the most enormous boobs, in a way, she is elegant, in a way deformed. She went to a very posh school but led, as far as I can divine, a rather sad life as a spinster. I find that hard to believe because she's such fun. She has no relations as far as I can see, apart from her musically accomplished niece, she seldom talks about family. – I often wonder why. Elisabeth is very religious, I'm not sure about me, I think I only go to prayers because Elizabeth does. I think she has designs on the Bishop Boyd.

The Bishop arrived about eighteen months ago, quite a kafuffle there was, he immediately became Elizabeth's personal confessor, though I suspect they just drink tea and gossip. The Bishop is not really a bishop but an ex-auxiliary bishop and an ex-army chaplain. He's a good looking man about eighty I suppose but I don't really know him. He's a shade untidy and spills his food down his tummy. I could never abide messy men.

I've had other friends, there was Milly, "A new day is always a lovely thing." That's what Milly said every morning. One morning she just didn't appear, we've not seen her since. McCann reported that Milly has "Gone". She left without fuss. People 'go' quite often, McCann likes them to go over at night, Mr Morgan and his assistants are adept at not waking us up.

After Lionel died, I decided that men were no longer an essential, in fact I felt relieved that

Lionel was gone. Despite his charm, I never got used to his constant control and his lack of caring intimacy. I remember trying to cry with his daughters, because I should have been grieving. Penny couldn't wait for the will, but Marie did appear to grieve for her Dad. One of his redeeming features was that he really did love his daughters, though some would say he spoiled them dreadfully. My prejudices were confirmed when I learned that the house we'd lived in, and which had absorbed a great deal of my original equity was left in trust for the girls. Fortunately other funds from Tim's pension and compensation allowed me to move on. I became one of the legions of the lost, it's funny how the world looks at widows and what we used to call spinsters as lonely odd balls.

I managed, did more than just manage, I enjoyed great swathes of my widowed existence partly because I gave a great deal of my time and attention to the Downs Syndrome Association charity where I made lots of friends both male and female. My only indiscretion was David from Leicester, now barely a memory.

The thing that brought Elizabeth and me together is music. She was, still is, an accomplished pianist, and I was once, a long time ago not a bad hand on the violin. Indeed as a young woman I was torn between studying medicine or music. My dear father was a Doctor and Mum a piano teacher and both were keen that I should follow their careers. Mum won and I went up to the Royal College of Music to study violin when I was just eighteen. I loved it, I loved London, I adored my teacher who was a handsome Frenchman, a descendant of Franz Louis Pique a great French violin maker of the eighteenth century. It was just after the war, times were tough but we had lots of fun making music and young women finding our way in the world. It seems so long ago now, the war had just ended and despite our paucity of riches we just had one wonderful time, making music and making our first real boy girl relationships.

We were all innocent, certainly by today's standards. I had lots of boyfriends all of whom were like little kittens. I never once felt that I'd been the subject of sexual exploitation. Seem to read of little else in the newspapers nowadays. I remember the lads trying it on as we used to say. If they were not one of my favourites they just got a light smack. Inevitably they retreated like the young gentlemen were.

I met Tim, at a student's dance in the Imperial College Union. He wasn't that much of a hit with me, to tell the truth. However, he persevered and we met with our other friends and I came to like him, eventually to love him, like I've never loved anyone else. Tim was a bit gawky, tall and awkward, he had lovely hair, and a sweet deep voice. It was his voice that I fell in love with. I still hear him now. Deep and gentle, firm and warm that was my Tim. He was four years older than me and doing his PhD in Civil Engineering. He wasn't very musical but he sat through all those awful concerts stoically pretending to enjoy himself.

Dad loved him from first sight, being a civil engineer was after all a proper job. Mum too took Tim to her heart. There was something special about how they welcomed him when he first appeared with suite case and polished shoes. I think my mum who was beginning to fail, like me, went for his lovely voice. Dad thought another Doctor in the family was good, even if he wasn't a medical man.

Elizabeth has never really relaxed and talked about her girl growing up history. I feel that her reserved nature and her rather sad and lonely adult life had something to do with her student experience. She never talks about her past and despite my almost constant chatter never really lets go. She's the original introvert. I like her so much and sometimes I want to squeeze her and help her share, yes that's the word, share a bit more of herself.

Apart from Dotty and Elizabeth, I have few friends. Elizabeth and I spend hours talking about music and books. Sometimes we gossip about the men. Colonel Henry was a real change and it was so sad that he died, so quickly. He even did that with a certain amount of swagger. His departure so sudden and in the common room was a shock to us all. There was a palpable intake of breath as everyone saw death march so emphatically into our modest afternoon. Apart from Colonel Henry's sudden departure we still had in our hours of gossip talked about the men, there are fewer of them than us ladies. I must say that, apart from Elizabeth, I find the ladies either silly, as if they've gone back to their childhood, or with nothing in common with me at all.

Among the men there is Brian who is so camp, he is quite lovely but very silly but silly in a sort of pantomimic way.. They tell me he was a very successful fashion designer, his gaudy cravats and kerchiefs belie his claims, at least, it seems to me. Then there's the Professor who I think is afraid of us ladies, tall and gaunt, he always has his head in a book or journal. He seems to be the judge and leader of the men, a certain gravitas attends him, perhaps more aloofness. His friend John who's such a sweetie and is like a little sparrow with a broken leg. John has not long arrived, he seems shy and a bit sad. There is something about him I find vulnerable, when I look at him, I often think of my long lost little boy. There have been others and I can't remember many of them, Dan who's gone, and Nigel who has lost all his marbles and talks about golf to anyone who will listen.

Elizabeth and I pass much time talking about this motley crew of ancient manhood, I cannot but help looking and then imagining their pasts. Despite all these curiosities I am quietly content. Please God I continue with my health.

Chapter20

Everyone here who still is compos mentis is aware that we could expire at any time, Colonel Henry had reminded us so emphatically.. This is the great elephant in the room. In all the rooms I'm sure. We defend, or at least I do, by living in the past. Tim and Bernie are with me most days, sometimes for a minute some times for all of the day.

Sometimes I babble on about my latest book or some music I've heard on the wireless. Elizabeth, though is much quieter, she remains very much within herself. She occasionally breaks out into enthusiastic responses to my musical asides. We are about the only ones I know who listen virtually exclusively to Radio 3. Then on other occasions Elizabeth sits, tight-lipped like the Sphinx whilst I ramble on.

It was a surprise therefore when she just came out with, "What do you think about dying? Do you think we should manage our own exits?"

"Darling girl, of course I do, we all do, but never thought about dying except in a rather abstract way…as in. ' it's going to happen, I hope not tonight… you know when we get aches and pains I think about it, we're all going to go Elizabeth, let's not worry about it, that's all."

"The men are talking about an assisted dying club." Elizabeth said this in the lowest tone, I could hardly hear her.

Silence.

"Brian he told me, they're going to have a meeting, Brian said we could go. I'd like to go, will you come with me?"

My breath was knocked out of me, what was Elizabeth talking about – A suicide club, whatever are they thinking about? It was my turn to be quiet, I suppose Colonel Henry has something to do with this new wave of thought. I can't believe Brian is the fount of this initiative, the man is a fop, he may have designed some dresses, but founding an assisted dying club is something not in his sphere.

"Shall we have a cup of tea dear?"

It must be the idea of dear Mr John Betts, he's been through such a hard time lately, he fell and I tried to visit him when he was recovering. I used the Professor as my intermediary, it was all so sad. Poor Mr Betts not only with his crippled leg but now a bad shoulder as well. In some ways I wish I hadn't bothered, he was very short and grumpy, but I still felt a little for him. He's so lucky he can afford a full time Carer that strange little man Tomos.

"I think Mr Betts may be the man, Elizabeth, surely not Brian. I will try and see him, I think we should tread carefully."

In my room, I take Abigail down from her safe wardrobe, I open the case and my old violin 'Abigail' shines up at me. She is old and valuable, I have not played her for fifteen years or more. She has a wonderful sound, and she is so beautiful as to almost defy description. Over the years she has been my refuge against grief, cruelty and confusion. When I look at her, particularly her burnished back, I can still hear her. Like all young musicians I believed I would be amongst the greatest, and despite my promising start 'Abi' was never played on the greatest of stages. My dreams of being a star soloist were just swept away by my love affair with Tim. Still 'Abi' remains untainted by any of the ups and downs of my life. Bernie loved me playing from Bach to Beatles,

He would reach for 'Abi' and he knew instinctively what a wondrous violin 'Abi' was and still is. Tim used to hold Bernie on his lap and they would both listen to me play, they were the world's most distinguished audience, for them I played with all my heart and soul. Those musical moments were by far the most satisfying of my musical life.

"John Betts" there's a challenge, he's a strange man, I can't make up my mind about him, nor can I understand why I care. But and it's a big 'but' I do seem to care, maybe it's his limp, maybe it's his shyness, whatever? I will try to enter his assisted suicide club, not even he can be really that miserable.

I put 'Abi' back in her lovely warm case, gather myself together and march out in search of John Betts. He is nowhere to be seen, but Alex tells me which is his room. I tap on the door, there is a shuffle and he opens the door. It's as if he's seen a ghost, his shyness overcomes him. He does not invite me in, he is very formal. He calls me Madame, I suppress a laugh and we stroll to the conservatory where he vehemently denies any knowledge about assisted suicide or any other sort of suicide.

Since then I have got to know John a good deal better, he's a lamb really. We were invited to the Professors 'exit' club and we listened to the

Professor give us chapter and verse on how to do away with ourselves. John during the first meeting was quiet and I enjoyed being beside him I didn't think for a moment that he was going to be an enthusiastic 'do it yourselfer.'

I have become quite fond of him and I was profoundly saddened at the second meeting when he offered to be our first assisted suicide. It was a shocking moment. My instant response was to invite him to take lunch with me. The gesture surprised me as much as it surprised John. I am pleased, I think, and tomorrow I must make an effort to cheer him up. How can I lift his melancholy? I must give him something to look forward to. I must make him want to believe in tomorrow, I suppose that means I must make him want to be my friend. We all have to have somebody. John has made me realise that perhaps I need somebody too. I will be his friend but I will also be his ticket to go out, he will hate that because I still have my green wrist band, John is no longer allowed out unescorted.

I am in a state of anxiety, dates at eighty are not things that happen every day. I hope John is happy about our lunch tomorrow. I feel nearer eighteen than eighty, I am shaking, not sure with excitement or fear. I take down Abi from her case and I hear her and Tim, "Go for it, enjoy!" What shall I wear? I mustn't be too early, I mustn't be too late, I must be careful not to put on too much make up.

It's Elizabeth, bless her. I must try not be too excitable. What can we talk about?

"My dear Patricia, how kind you are, rescuing poor old Betts from making a complete fool of himself."

"Shall we see who's in the conservatory? "

"What do you think it'll be like when you have lunch with him tomorrow? Would you like me to join you?

I feel myself going scarlet, can Elizabeth be so insensitive? I cannot think, what shall I say? I'd like to say 'don't be so stupid', I'd like to say 'John Betts needs somebody and I need somebody' but I say nothing hoping Elizabeth will shut up or change the subject.

"I think it would be a good idea if I joined you both, you never know how men can be."

"Look Elizabeth, I think Mr.Betts needs a quiet chat, he's obviously depressed or he wouldn't have put himself forward to, you know …end things."

"But you never know Patricia, men can be very unpredictable."

The evening drags, my patience is severely tested but at last Elizabeth changes the subject and talks of her nieces' next musical adventure. The night is a long one. When at last we say goodnight I sit for ages thinking about what I will wear, I hardly sleep a wink.

241

Chapter 21　　　　John

I have hardly slept a wink, last night was so
embarrassing, I can't think what made me jump
up like a fool and volunteer to do myself in. I
have always had an impatient temper, and lots of
things conspired to make me want to make a
grand gesture. Underneath it all were two things,
dear old Dan, and HB carrying on with
'Oddsocks'. Anyway, that's what I thought at
the time.

Then HB of all people stood and invited me for
lunch today, how astonishing, I am reduced to
chaotic emotions; does she like me? Why did
she make such a gesture? Does she feel guilty?
How am I to respond, I don't know what to do. I
tried hard this morning to talk to Margaret and
Johanna but they remain obdurately silent. Last
night in bed, I rehearsed a hundred times, what I
must say and how I must behave. I must not
take that ridiculous Zimmer contraption. I must
shave as neatly as I can, I know lately my

shaving has been untidy. I shall wear my blazer and regimental tie. I must remember to put on enough deodorant, I don't want to smell like a barber's shop.

This morning Tomos has brought in a message reminding me that we are to be ready for a taxi at the main entrance at noon. Tomos notices immediately my anxiety. He reads the note and is on the ball straight away.

My shoes, my shoes, they always give me away, bloody cripple that I am. Tomos fusses and polishes my boot and corresponding shoe. I suddenly become aware that the colours do not quite match.

"Put some more brown polish on there's a good chap", but it makes no difference. At eleven fifteen I am ready, I look in the mirror, "Don't look so bad for an eighty five year old." Who am I kidding? I look old and stooping. I remember Sergeant Major Lloyd, 'Stand up straight, neck into your collar, stomach in, legs straight. I try my best, oh dear! I have to go to the bathroom. The whole rigmarole will have to start again.

There is a knock on the door and in breezes McCann,, "Good morning John, just popped up to change your wrist band, we don't want to have to register, do we?"

Christ everyone knows about my appointment with HB, I feel as if I'm back in boarding school and teacher is giving me a note out, "Thankyou Joan, that's most considerate." I see the palpable relief on Tomos's face. So far I'm being good.

Down at the main entrance, my apprehension is so great that I consider turning back, but Tomos is close and gently behind me. There is no turning back. And there she is, HB, she looks fabulous in pale blue, she has a short jacket and pearl ear rings and a delicate pearl necklace. She looks stunning. I have quite forgotten Sergeant Major Lloyd, I slump on my walking stick, my mouth may well be hanging open.

"Hello John you look really smart." She puts out her hand, I let in fall into mine and put it gently to my lips.

"Dear lady, you look beautiful." I feel the tears come to my eyes. I have not felt like this for eternity. I am full of pride and joy, and the tears roll down my face. HB to her everlasting credit, mops them away, "shall we go," she says, "the taxi is waiting."

'The Moon and Sixpence' is a lovely old pub, I have no idea what to expect. It is rather grand inside and we are shown to a table for two overlooking the garden. Once more I am covered in confusion, it's a bit like my first date seventy years ago. Should I pay? Of course.

"It's very nice to be out and about," I say, "what a nice place, how did you find it?"

HB peers at me round her menu, "John, why did you do it? Whatever made you say you want to be dead? You shocked us all, Why John, why?"

"I wanted you to invite me to lunch." My flippant reply misses the mark. The object of my desire humphs and her attention returns to the menu.

"It's not funny John, not funny at all."

"Garlic prawns, look nice."

She puts down the menu, HB stares at me, she is flushed with anger, I am very uncertain of what to do. "John, am I wasting my time?"

I really do not know what to say. I remain silent, staring at the menu which I cannot see through my awkward embarrassment. I must try. I stammer, and stutter, "Please HB, I am flattered that you rescued me from my silly self. You have no idea how depressed I've been, just thought I was of no use to anybody especially you. I am so sorry my dear."

"John, I am in some danger of not being 'your dear' as you put it. Why are you so obdurately stupid and unseeing? I will say this for the last time, I think I like you and I think you like me. Is that the case John?"

Again I am dumb, was not HB canoodling with 'Oddsocks'? Did she not spend time with Geoff behind my back? Does it matter that she did?

"John, I'm waiting."

"I thought you liked the Professor, I thought you had a thing going with him,…. I thought you didn't care to see me or spend time with me, I'm sorry, perhaps we shouldn't have come here."

HB is now really angry, she thrusts down her napkin, shoos the waiter away. "I can barely stand the Professor, he's an introverted bookworm as far as I am concerned. I came with him to see you because I thought it would be more appropriate to visit you with a male escort, at least whilst you were in bed. How incredibly silly you are John, totally insensitive. Shall we have a drink?"

247

My nervousness is quickly turned to euphoria, I reach across the table and take her hand, "I think two gin and tonics and lots of time together would be the most wonderful thing – ever!"

She laughs and we spend the next two hours talking of voices and Johanna and Tim, David and Bernie, and violins and Dotty and Abigail. Time passes in a flash. On the taxi ride back to Swallow House I am happier than I have been for many years. This beautiful girl of eighty or so has made my heart bound out of my chest. I can hardly stop myself from laughing with the delight of this sparkling new life. Yes, it is a new life. I hold her lovely hand in mine, she does not object but gently squeezes and the softest of caresses surges through my old body, dare I say it, reaching places I thought long dead.

We separate at the door, like two children each going his/her way guiltily pretending that nothing has happened. Something certainly has happened and I can't wait for tomorrow when

HB is going to introduce me to Abi. I must say I wasn't at all clear about who Abi is, something to do with her grandmother. I am also in line to meet her other best chum Doctor Dotty, didn't quite get that either. As far as I'm concerned I know how easily things can change. I know too that I am a bit impatient, so I must be careful to embrace this wonderful gift of affection and not do anything silly.

"Mr. Betts how was your date? Everyone is talking about you and the nice lady, you look like you had good time – yes."

"Don't be impertinent Tomos I merely had lunch with the admittedly very nice Mrs Hayes Bowen, we went to The Moon and Sixpence, it was very nice. And that's all you're going to get out of me Tomos, You are not to gossip with the other staff…do you understand?"

"Oh yes, very nice lady for you Mr Betts I am very happy for you, very nice lady, I see her, she very nice."

"Tomos, are you deaf, did you hear what I just said?"

Tomos taps his nose, "I keep secret, Mr Betts has nice woman."

I find it impossible to be cross today, There is a knock on the door and Brian is there smelling slightly of gin. "I say my love, how did it go?"

"How did what go? For Christ's sake Brian I just had lunch with HB that's all, she chastised me about the meeting that's all."

There's another knock on my door this time it's Geoff, "how did it go old boy?"

"Oh bollocks, Geoff you'll tell me next the bloody bishop will be next."

"Well we all want to know if she persuaded you to step back from an early exit/"

At which point, Brian invited us all to the conservatory for a drink, where no doubt the rest of the inmates of this mad house will come and gawp. There is much bonhomie, and back slapping, it only then occurs to me that these friends are celebrating my recovery from my stupid rash and extremely wild offer to do myself in. Indeed, no sooner are we settled into a quiet corner of the conservatory, the Professor launches into a lecture about avoiding emotional eccentricities and having safeguards if we are to continue with the 'Peaceful pill' group.

I am humbled by their concern, and maybe for the first time since I've been in Swallow house I believe I have friends who care for me, that I matter to them. I don't quite know how to respond, my tongue is for once tied I try to melt unseen into their collective affection.

Chapter 22   'HB'

I have barely taken off my jewellery when there is a hasty urgent knocking on my door. It is Elizabeth, "Dear Girl, Patricia did he behave himself, was he wild?"

"What do you mean, was he wild? Of course he wasn't wild. In fact he was rather sweet. He's a bit ashamed of himself, he didn't really want to kill himself, he just wanted some attention I think."

"Well I think you took a big risk, he is after all a manic depressive with suicidal tendencies."

"Elizabeth, you're talking non sense, I agree he's been a bit depressed, but he's had a bad time poor dear with his fall and his disability, he only sees his son about two or three times a year, and bless him, like the rest of us, he's found it hard to settle down. Anyway he has a lovely voice and he paid for lunch."

"You make excuses for him Patricia, he is just a miserable man who cannot be trusted." Her voice betrayed a wound that ran deep. Was this why Elizabeth was so detached, some man in her past? God knows I have the reason to dislike men, but Lionel was not all men and then there are men like Tim, my lovely Tim. Or for that matter Dave from Leicester wasn't a bad man either.

Elizabeth immediately changes the conversation, there is no doubt that the male sex is a very sensitive subject as far as she is concerned. She prattles on about nothing at all. I hate to say it but I'd like to leave me. I'd like to enjoy the memories of this afternoon. John Betts, oh, John Betts you've quite stolen my heart. He is such a vulnerable man, his disability and his frail frame after his fall, his loneliness and his hankering for the past. I think he still grieves for his wives, what a good man he must be to have loved then both so intensely.

Elizabeth is still prattling on. "Excuse me Elizabeth darling, but I must go to the bathroom and have a nap. She leaves reluctantly, why can't I feel more sympathy for her?

As soon as she leaves I get Abigail down from her safe place, I open up her warm home and marvel at how beautiful she is. I can hear her sing, she is a soaring soprano and a sonorous contralto. When I played at my best she was part of me. My teacher said we could sing a vibrato like a hummingbird, we could make the sky sound brighter, oh! they were such great days. I could never let Abigail go, but now I must, for she's worth a small fortune and she should be played by someone full of music and a lust for life. There are several foundations out there that will take Abi and give her a new life with some deserving young musician. Abi can live for ever, she can move many to tears of joy, Abi will sing long after I've gone.

I'll show her to John Betts, he loves music I know. I hope that Abigail will enchant him and that he will see in us both the loveliness that we both have shared. Can I let her go? I think I must, if only John will keep me company whilst I think of her, hear her and see her in my mind's eye. I think I'm being ridiculously romantic, how long will we be?

Abi has been my rock even in the awful times with Lionel, at least I was a musician, quite a good one. I taught lots of nice kids, I played in small bands, made music with the Downs Syndrome Association. I performed a few solos with amateur orchestras, I did some session work in Southampton, and played many times with the Bournemouth Symphony. I could do things that the Bowen clan could not and that kept me balanced against Penny's nasty sniping and Lionel's controlling fetishes.

Abigail is a name not everyone would associate with a violin. But 'Abi' was my Grandma's name and it was she who gifted this fabulous violin to me when I went up to the Royal College where she, the violin, was the object of much envy.

Before I make the break I will introduce 'Abi' to John, I do hope he finds her as ravishing as I do. If he can share her with me then we can both let her go, that will ease the pain that will be inevitable. 'Abi' was born in 1840 to 50 made by a very famous maker named George Chanot. She is a fabulous example of a Guaneri copy by great French master of the 19th century. She is fabulous to just look at, The varnish, still original and untouched, has lumps and bumps, she carries the fake label of Joseph Guanerius, which Chanot did a lot. Not to fake it, but to show faith with the Cremona tradition. I don't suppose John will want to know any of this, but I cannot forget the look on my teacher's Monsieur Pique's face the first time he saw and heard me play in the Royal College. I believe that 'Abi' is so beautiful to touch and to behold, that John will understand my admittedly strange love affair with my violin.

Elizabeth knocks insistently on the door. "Yes what is it?"

"I've been thinking about that man Betts, I think you're in real danger." She looks a bit unhinged, she's staring at me and makes me feel very uncomfortable. Against my better judgement I ask her in. I hastily put Abi away.

"Now, Elizabeth what is all this about?" Suddenly Elizabeth seems to be uncontrollable, she will not stop, she is mumbling and rambling about men. I think I hear her father mentioned, then it seems Elizabeth sinks into a very black mood. I do not quite know what to do, "Would you like a cup of tea?"

"Yes, yes, that would be nice but these men they are all disgusting, we need to be very careful, don't let them in, no don't let them in."

"In where?", I make the tea, something is terribly wrong. I make an instant decision and press my alarm bell. Poor Elizabeth is very unwell."

I serve the tea, gently as I can, Elizabeth is looking into the middle distance, "The Bishop, he is the only man we can trust, keep them away Patricia, keep them away"

She drinks her tea, then amazingly, seems to return to normal, at the same time Alex rushes in – "The alarm,! What's the problem?"

"Oh, nothing really, Elizabeth was a little unwell."

"Unwell, dear I'm fine."

I make eyes that I hope Alex understands, he sees my plea. Elizabeth drinks her tea, Alex is about to go and I plead for him to stay I almost push a cup and saucer at him. He sees my anxiety.

In desperation "Excuse us Elizabeth there's something Alex and I have to discuss would you mind."

"Not at all, dear." She gets up a little unsteadily and leaves Alex and I alone.

"What is it Mrs Hayes-Bowen? What's up?"

"I'm not sure how to put this Alex, call me Patricia, please, but Elizabeth behaved in a very strange way, that's why I pressed the emergency button, I'm very sorry, but honestly she was very very out of character, she sort of went off about men. At first I thought she maybe a bit funny about me having lunch yesterday with Mr Betts, but she really went off the deep end about men, about how they threatened us, about her father, really scary, very odd and very unlike Elizabeth."

"Miss Wainwright has been with us a good while and she's your good friend, so tell me in detail what you think is wrong."

An hour later McCann asks that we all go to her office following Alex's report. I go through the whole story once again. Miss Wainwright and her condition are discussed without any further input from myself. McCann thanks me and tells me I did the right thing calling Alex.

I go back to my rooms, I want to talk to someone, I would like to talk to dear John, but I dare not, I will speak to him tomorrow. Tomorrow is now a mess, I was so looking forward to introducing John to Abi, but dare I bring him to my rooms, will Elizabeth be watching?

I must pull myself together, come on Patricia, Elizabeth has always been a bit odd and introverted. This outburst about men in general and John in particular maybe just an 'episode'. She has been my closest friend for a long time now since Milly passed. I shall pop in and see her.

"Hello Elizabeth, may I come in?"

"Of course, Patricia, shall we go over to the conservatory for a sherry?"

"Good idea, let's do that." Elizabeth is right as rain. Maybe her 'episode' was just that.

Bishop Boyd we learn is not well and has been admitted to the infirmary. Elizabeth is beside herself, she gets into a flap, and insists she will go and see Mr Boyd in the morning. I enquire when? That will be my time to invite John to meet Abi. Elizabeth seems quite normal again, I am quietly pleased.

It seems that Bishop Boyd has been unwell for some time, he has been dropping things and he has fallen several times. The gossip is running in a torrent. Boyd has been our minister and confidante for some time. You either love him or loathe him. I was never sure about him but Elizabeth has always worshipped the ground he walks on. I have no idea why? Maybe it's a religious thing. Personally I don't like Boyd's singing almost whining voice. Each to her own I suppose.

It seems an age since John and I had our lunch together and even longer to the meeting of the peaceful pill brigade. I remain excited and I'm not sure why. I don't understand why I have taken a liking to John or why for that matter why he's taken to me. Any way tomorrow will soon come 'god willing' and John will help me, I'm sure, to decide on Abi's future. Before I go to sleep I spring out of bed and get Abi down and open up her case, she smiles up at me and reminds me too of her special partners, my bows. I have three one of which I'm told is more valuable than the other two. In my playing days this bow by 'August Barbe' was always 'the other one', I used him on odd occasions when I felt my playing was out of sorts. 'Barbe' always brought me back to my best, but for or some reason I always reverted to my other bows. People who have never played the violin have no idea how important the bow is. As you lay it on the strings there comes a sound that can be perfect or less so. Therein lies the art of playing the violin. Let me sleep, tomorrow shines on the horizon, let the lights dim, Bernie, Tim and John will all gather in my heart to make the best of Abi's future, we must let her sing in someone's talented arms.

Chapter 23 'HB'

Breakfast in our dining room has always been a segregated affair, I'm not at all sure why. Eleanor Lewis (Mrs) and Miriam Davies (unknown) and of course Elizabeth join the table for breakfast. I cannot help peaking across the room to catch a sight of John Betts, alas, he doesn't appear. The professor and his pals are there, but John and Bishop Boyd are missing. I hope fervently that John is well.

Elizabeth seems herself, very quiet as usual, Eleanor and Miriam chatter on about nothing at all. The Bishop is according to them near his maker. Elizabeth is visibly upset, I can see her trying to restrain her anxiety, but tears roll from beneath her glasses. By the way I am the only one who doesn't need glasses and I'm rather proud of that fact. I had a cataract op four years ago and I've had very good vision since, though I do need reading glasses. Elizabeth leaves the table without ceremony, Eleanor seems unperturbed whilst Miriam looks surprised. "I think she's got a soft spot for Boyd", she says.

John Betts emerges and looks really smart, he smiles at me and I feel a slight shiver and I smile back. It feels rather more like a grimace, I hope he doesn't see it as such. Eleanor and Miriam are engaged in a detailed discussion about knitting, this is something that leaves me cold, I have never knitted anything in my life. The clothes for Bernie were I'm afraid either given to us or purchased. The ladies get up to leave still deeply engaged in the problems of wool and knitting, I dwell on my cold tea, then as the ladies leave John Betts makes his way as elegantly as he can, I see him straining to be up right and not lean too hard on his walking stick. He looks quite elegant in a very nice buttoned cardigan. His smile is nervously set, I pretend I don't see his approach.

"Good morning HB, I hope this morning finds you in the best of health."

"Good morning John, yes, thankyou I am quite well thank you, would you like me to curtsey? Why are we being so formal? Have you finished your breakfast because, as I promised, I want you to come and meet Abi."

We make our way, quietly with no words, I can feel the tension, I do hope John is not going to do anything silly, he can be silly. As I get to my door I put these fears out of my mind. The cleaning lady is just finishing off in my rooms. She casts a look of amused suspicion and leaves, her plastic bucket and other cleaning accoutrements making something of a clatter. She leaves the door open behind her. I close it with a firm clunk.

John is standing with his back to me, he seems quite frozen to the spot. "Sit down John, would you like a cup of tea?"

"No, no, I'm fine." He sits walking stick under his chin and between his awkwardly asymmetric legs. Poor lamb, I can see what a huge problem his crippled leg is for him, he looks embarrassed I mustn't delay, I half expect Elizabeth to come charging in with news of Boyd's demise.

"Now John, what do you know about violins?"

He says nothing, then "Um, not a lot really I like to listen to them of course."

"Well you do remember me telling you that I used to play one, pretty well, you remember me telling you I studied music and the violin in particular?"

John is clearly uncomfortable, I suspect he paid no attention at all, does he remember anything of yesterday?

"Of course I do, I remember very well you played to your lovely little boy, Brian…..no Bernie, of course I remember."

Is this what old age is about? Meeting someone you really like, then struggling to remember what you are all about? My heart sinks a little, I must get Abi down and commit to my little dream. If John responds, he responds, if he doesn't, well so be it. Without another word I get Abi down and open the case and lay it on the coffee table in front of John. I take Abi out and lay her free from her case, and I lay my three bows above her. I stand back. There is a long silence. Does he know what he's looking at? Please, please, John say something.

"HB, that's one of the most lovely things I've ever seen, look at that colour, my goodness it is, sorry, Abi is very beautiful, nearly as beautiful as you." He is weeping.

I take his hands and raise him up and we embrace. I am beyond words. We are both weeping ponds full of tears. I can smell him, he is sweet and clean and warm. I am in a clinch for the first time for years and years and it is lovely. I am wrapped in happiness, and for the first time since Tim died I think I am in love.

We separate and I kiss him on his cheek. John fishes out a tissue and blows his nose, "HB" he mutters, "HB I don't know what to say except thank you, and hello Abi", he blows his nose and sits again. "Will you play her? He asks.

"No John, I will not play her, she is too good for me, maybe she was always too good for me. Anyway old hands and fingers are well passed their playing days." The next hour passes as I launch into what I know and love about Abigail and her assorted bows. I outline to John what I think the ensemble is worth and how I would like to put Abi in trust for a new young artist. He doesn't say a word, he is wrapped in my every word.

At last, he says very quietly, "HB I know nothing of violins but I would be honoured if you let me help with the research and options for your lovely Abi, let's see what the options are."

It is nearly lunchtime, John suggests we eat together, I'm delighted by the suggestion, though I know there will be much gossiping and whispering, who cares, I don't! John Betts, Abi and me, we are family, well nearly family. At that point, the door bursts open and Elizabeth bursts in, she stops, looks at John, bursts into tears and blurts out,

"How dare you, you bitch, Bishop Boyd is very sick and here you are carrying on with, with this cripple!"

I see the colour drain from John's face, "I'd better go", he says. Elizabeth has hit him where it hurts him most. All the warmth goes out of the room, I look down, I hold John's hand.

"No John, stay. Elizabeth please, leave us now, I'm sorry about the Bishop, but please, leave us now". Elizabeth turns and slams the door behind her. In the cold quiet I embrace John, "You are a very sweet and lovely man" I whisper in his ear. I can fccl him tremble in my arms, he is trying not to cry.

"Come," let's go into lunch, I want us to continue our chat about Abi." John pulls himself straight. He is trying very hard to absorb the 'the cripple' barb, trying with all his courage to just ignore it. I don't know what to say, then for no reason at all, I blurt out, "Come on hop-a-long you're my favourite man."

I almost close my eyes in shock, but to my delight, John takes my arm, "Yes," he says you're my favourite lady too." With that, we walk, as up right as we can be, arm in arm to the dining room. We sit together on a table for four. The room goes absolutely quiet, you can hear a pin drop.

A helper comes and fills our water glasses, offers us as usual the choice of two lunch options. We reply firmly our voices almost echoing off the dining room walls. Then the muttering and chattering resumes. Elizabeth enters, and with great ceremony, makes an almost audible humph, and sits alone.

I look at John, he nods and I go over and invite her to join us. She refuses even to speak.

Another silence. I sit with John and smile at him. We can both feel the tension. It is broken by Brian who joins us with a cheery, "Hello darlings, what's for dins today."

As the days slip by, John and I stick together, we have a wonderful lunch out with Dotty, and John has done a great deal of research (with the help of his man Tomos) and as a result a gentleman is coming down from Bonham's to value Abi, and we expecting two visits from instrument trusts. All in all, it's very exciting.

Grandma Abigail Forster gave me the violin in 1950 and even then it was very valuable, my father went to great lengths about insurance and lectured me about looking after her. The 'August Barbe' bow was given to me by Grandpa Forster when I graduated. I played at both their funerals, memories that still make me tear up.

Mr. Fairburn from Bonham's arrived on Wednesday, we all assembled courtesy of

McCann in the office meeting room. John, Dotty and I sat together with Anna Bryan, Harry's daughter who now runs the firm and my trust affairs. Mr. Fairburn is tall, very well dressed and I could not help but notice his lovely polished shoes, he was accompanied by a lovely young lady called Joe.

"I am given to understand "said Fairburn "that you have a well preserved and presented violin attributed to George Chanot circa 1840."

John intervened, "Sir, you are not given to understand, we have the violin here, there is no doubt."

Fairburn smiled, "We shall see" he says, "May I?" He opened up Abi's case and took her out. He didn't say a word as he examined her in gentle detail. I thought I might burst with the tension, Dotty smoothed my back, John held his walking stick as his knuckles went white.

The minutes ticked by, still Fairburn uttered not a word. After an interminable five minutes or so, he looked up mutters to the decorous Joe, who noted down some data, then he looked at me and said, "Do you have any documentation of provenance by chance?"

I have a lot of old papers relating to all the gifts from my grandparents, I went with Dotty back to my rooms where we fumble and fiddle with the papers seemingly in vain, when at last I remember they, the documents, insurance and old paper from my Grandparents are high in my wardrobe.

We go back to McCann's trying not to run, though running I must say is not my forte. Dotty hands the documents over, coffee is served whilst Fairburn again ignores us all and carefully goes through all the old papers. John is beside himself, he fidgets, and grunts every time Fairburn leafs through the pile of papers. Joe, his pretty secretary, is taking notes and photographs on her phone. There is unbearable tension.

After about forty minutes, Fairburn nods, and starts to restring the violin, all except the 'e' string are fine. He bows several notes, he is obviously very competent, he puts Abi down. "Mrs Hayes Bowen, can you tell me please who is Abigail Forster?"

"My grandmamma," I scratch an answer, my throat is dry despite the coffee.

"Hm, well I'm pleased to tell you that I can confirm that this violin is indeed a Georges Chanot, I think of 1840-5, it is immaculate, Mrs Hayes Bowen you are to be congratulated, it is in splendid condition and would grace any concert platform as is. I am happy with the provenance, it is just wonderful, …now as regards valuation, I would opine subject to a second opinion from my colleagues that the violin would fetch (£80,000) eighty thousand pounds at auction and the bows around ten to fifteen thousand pounds, the 'Barbe' alone should get ten thousand."

You could hear a pin drop. "Oh I said that's very nice, thank you very much."

Anna Bryan, the lawyer, "May I say this is just a little higher value than we expected and I think Patricia should have time to consider her options."

"Quite right." mutters John.

"What we shall do now is go back to London and make you a proposal for our next fine instrument auction, it has been a great pleasure." Fairburn stood and he and his secretary shook hands and left.

Silence, stunned silence, I knew Abi was valuable but little idea of her true worth. John was the first to speak, "Well, bless my soul, dear Abi is worth a fortune, congratulation HB, fantastic news."

"Yes, yes it is, but what shall I do, such a lot of worth."

"Nothing, now at least, let's all think about what you want to do Patricia, there are so many options, I think you should wait for Bonham's formal written valuation and then decide." Anna shuffled in her seat. "May I have a word alone with my client please."

"No", I said, "I trust John and Dotty implicitly, we can discuss anything, I have nothing to hide, besides I think I'll want all the advice I can get, dear old Abi what a lovely surprise and what shall I do?"

"Are you sure HB? I don't mind pushing off, quite understand legal stuff and all that." John started to lift himself to his feet, not the simplest of manoeuvres.

"Oh sit down John, Don't be such a silly boy." John dutifully returned to his seated posture with much fiddling with his chair, stick and what not.

Anna asked again if I was ready to discuss her estate in front of her friends. Again I affirmed my position. Dotty this time tried to excuse herself, but I appealed to her, and she sat with some reluctance.

The eighty thousand or so from the sale of Abi, she said was neither here or there, I had plenty of financial sources. The Question before us was what and when I wanted to do with her, either the sold or donated Abi, I could afford to give the violin to a young artist foundation, I could sell it, I could give the proceeds to a young musician's fund, or to the Downs Syndrome Association.

Anna suggested we explore the young musicians options, and see what we felt was the best thing to do. We would all meet again in two weeks. I felt exhausted. "John take me to my rooms, I need a little nap, Dotty will you bring Abi, and off we trouped, an old lady, a limping but gallant ancient gentleman and the petite doctor Dotty.

Five days later the official valuation arrived together with astonishing fees for Fairburn's visit and of course the valuation. I know I am old fashioned but the fee was infinitely more than I had imagined. Anna seemed unsurprised, Eight thousand pounds seemed a great deal to me however. I won't repeat what John said, but then he can be vulgar at times.

Elizabeth Wainwright spied on all these goings-on, and otherwise deliberately snubbed me whenever we met. I just couldn't understand what I had done to so hurt her. She became more and more isolated, and the only thing she did do was constantly visit Bishop Boyd who I understood was failing. John went to see him regularly but only bumped into Elizabeth once. She muttered a prayer of exorcism or so John thought. Boyd according to John was failing fast. Suddenly Boyd had streams of visitors, form the clergy and the army, it was as if someone had let it be known that Boyd was on his way to his maker.

John and I in the meantime had lunch out every week. We took turns to pay, John always the perfect gentleman. We spent quite a lot of time in John's rooms where he had a super music centre. I took the disc of my early auditions (used to be a tape and Dotty had then had them magically turned into a CD) with the Bournemouth. I am still very proud of it. It included lots of things but I love the Massenet's Meditation. It was when John first heard it, that he realised what Abi and me were all about. He cried, poor dear, but I loved him for his compassion. I always thought Abi sounded so lovely I can't remember which bow I used.

Chapter 24   HB

John is a kind man and he spends time with Bishop Boyd every day. He tells me it's hard to get a slot to see the old boy due to the hordes of visitors who as it were, have massed on the horizon. John is quite attached to Bishop Boyd, not because he's been a Bishop but because he's been a soldier. As I get to know John more it is clear that he loved the army. I never quite understood how John injured his leg, he just mumbles about 'bloody silly sport' whatever that refers to, I have no idea.

Since John volunteered to be our guinea pig in the euthanasia club, all that nonsense seems to have melted away. Boyd is on his way to meet his maker, the Professor looks as if he'll live for ever, Elizabeth, appears to be losing her mind. What do we all need a suicide club for?

It seems an age ago since John made such a silly gesture, but I hope, no I know, that he wants to stay alive and be my friend. This attachment has

surprised both of us. It's unlike anything I've
known before. Of course we're really old
fogeys, I don't think John or I want to do
anything vaguely to do with sex. The idea of
removing ones clothes and struggling to copulate
is too hideous to contemplate. I think John feels
the same, at least I do hope so. But despite all
that I do find John attractive, he has the sweetest
smile, a really impish grin and of course he has a
lovely voice. At the same time his battles with
his leg and his recent shoulder problem make
him so vulnerable I can't stop myself from
giving him a cuddle. It's all a bit coy I suppose,
but for me it's the new spring, just as exciting as
when I was a young girl, this time though there's
no hormones racing which makes everything so
much more gentle and relaxed. Dear John, I
hope he shares some of my feelings, I know he
likes me, I just hope I don't disappoint him in
any way.

One of the great gifts we have for each other is
the sharing of our lost loves. I don't talk about

Lionel at all, or his beastly children, but we spend hours and hours holding hands and remembering Bernie, or Tim, or Margret or Johanna, John's life came to an end when Johanna passed away. It seems he lived in a dark place and he only kept himself together for the sake of his son David. David and his family are another great love of John's and I'm excited to be meeting David in the coming weeks. John is anxious about it, I know, though he doesn't say so. He's afraid that David won't like me, I can't imagine why? If he's half the man his dad says he is, he will like me even if that's not the case, he will like me for his Dad's sake. I shall do my best, but if David is a little like his father I shall adore him. Now, I am just a little bit nervous, and my nerves will increase as David's visit gets nearer.

John's shoulder is much improved, I don't know how he would manage without Tomos, who's the most delightful young man. His language is sometimes lurid, but for all that he is genuinely fond of John. They have secret boys' jokes, they snigger together, but I don't mind. When I visit John in his rooms Tomos, bows as if I were royalty he calls me "Mrs. Aitchbee," he makes a lovely cup of coffee, and disappears but apparently never out of earshot. No idea how he does it. John and I are so comfortable together, we meet most days, go out for lunch once a week, and of course meet to discuss Abi's fate. I'm so pleased Dotty approves of John, they get on well together.

We are looking forward to the visit of a man from 'The loan fund for musical instruments' and the 'Cherubim Foundation.' We have also received calls from Bonham's who want to auction Abi, but many others too. It is really exciting and a challenge for me, John is always there supporting whatever idea comes into my head, but at the same time steering me gently to consensus with Dotty and Anna Bryan.

Spring is moving to summer, I have not been well, just a series of chills and headaches. We have reached a decision on Abi, she is to be given to an instrument foundation, who will keep us informed of her progress from there. We all hope we can meet the young man or woman who will be Abi's next lover.

John had been good apart from a few sniffles, he's improved a great deal and his arm is now almost back to normal. I am so proud of him, he's worked so hard in physio, been a tower of strength with me and kept peace with Elizabeth Wainwright who seems terminally deranged. Bishop Boyd is still with us and John tries to see him as often as he can, it seems Boyd is not letting go easily, he's been in the infirmary for going on three months, John says he's about to be moved to the Hospice. I never really had a relationship with Boyd but he must have been a nice gentleman because Elizabeth was devoted to him and he was much liked and respected by all the gentlemen especially John.

Unlike Boyd the turnover of ladies has continued at its usual pace, no fuss for them, just gone. There is always a waiting list for accommodation at Swallow House. In they come and out they go in an almost imperceptible continuum. I know my time is coming, I hold on to John, he is my reason now to be.

The excitement of David's thrice delayed visit is upon us. John has been twitchy for days, we've spent hours deciding how and when I am to be introduced. John assures me he has talked to David about me/us many times. David is coming on a flying visit, he now lives in California, so it's a really long haul.

At breakfast, John is looking lovely, Tomos has turned him out like a new pin. I can hardly stop myself from throwing my arms about my lovely man.

"David will be here around ten thirty, we usually spend a little time with McCann, say half an hour," Tea dribbles down his pristine shirt.

"Oh John, please be careful, look at you ." I
press forward and try to undo the tea stain in
vain.

"I expect David will want a chat in my rooms,
then I'll call for you to go to lunch, we'll go to
the Moon, if that's Ok with you?"

"Of course it is darling, but I won't mind if you
want to go, just the two of you, you don't see
David that often."

"No, you must come, I've told David about my
lovely HB, so you must come."

David is the most charming young man, much of
his dad about him. He is young, strapping and
handsome. He's a young forty something and he
treats me with such sweet courtesy, I
immediately feel he's part of us, John and me.
Our lunch is perhaps the happiest thing since
John and I first dallied hear an age ago. There is
no awkwardness, no silent gaps. I am so happy
to hear of all their family gossip about Shanta

and the children. I can feel the love between father and son, but they do not freeze me out, the embrace me, and I feel so warm and comforted.

Our goodbye is almost frantic, I want to hold these two in one big hug, but of course I cannot. I must be brave and make this parting sweet sorrow, how heart breaking it is. I feel John's heart bursting with pride and sorrow, we all cry. David so sweetly hugs me and holds both my hands in his.

"You are the best thing for Dad since Mum died, I do believe he'll make a hundred with you by his side. Love him and we'll all love you." With that, he kissed me on my forehead and turned and left, John and I, blessed, and even more together than ever.

Chapter25.   'HB'

Unusually, a notice goes up on the notice board announcing the death of Bishop Boyd. I have a slight feeling of anger, ladies come and ladies go and no one seems to care. I suppose the Bishop was an important figure in his way, but an announcement is still most unusual and in my opinion not called for.

John, is visibly upset. That surprises me too, maybe I'm jealous of John's other friends. I don't know what to think. In the notice attention is drawn to the Bishop's funeral and Swallow house will arrange transport. Again I am astonished. It seems the men will all go including John. I certainly won't, funerals are occasions I really want to avoid. For me, Patricia Hayes, every day is a blessing now that I have John Betts as my …. What is he? My boyfriend, absurd, my suitor… absurd, well maybe not so absurd. Do I love him? Yes I think I do, and that is why I don't want anything to do with funerals.

Being 'old' is an uncomfortable fact of life. Most of us here, sleep toward our inevitable end. All the ladies, at least those who are fit, talk about insignificant rubbish and almost always end up referring to our younger days. The thing is, we ladies can throw ourselves into these silly details and enjoy the minutes as they pass. Sometimes I compare my youth with the youth of others and know how lucky I've been. Sometimes we chatter on and I drift away and for the life of me I cannot recall what it is we are talking about.

When I am with John, we talk about our pasts with such joy. I love to hear about his marriages and his child's history. He listens wrapped in the adventure of my musical youth and with the heat of my devotion to Bernie and later the DSA. These times together are so different from how life was just a few months ago, in some wys I cannot believe what a change has been wrought by our coming together.

Today we had our first real row. John wants me to accompany him to Boyd's funeral, I have said no and I mean no.

"John, you can go with the boys' club, I think it's obscene that they are making such a fuss about Boyd, I have no intention of going so please, stop trying to push me, don't start, don't push, behaving like Lionel!"

John is upset and turns away. I am at once sorry but relieved that I stood my ground. I know I have said the wrong thing, completely uncalled for. John looks as if I've poked him in the eye with a sharp stick. He almost crumples in front of me. He turns without a word and marches off hobbling as best he can. I am sad, but I am cross. I am cross about the whole Boyd funeral affair it is in my view entirely wrong. And that is an end of it. John I'm sure will understand when he has time to reflect. My blood pressure has leapt, I am shaking with regret and angst, I am unsure and cross with myself. Nevertheless, my point was well made, I will not be pushed about by men. Lionel was enough. John, oh John, please say you're sorry.

At supper I sit with the ladies, I note that John Betts has not come down for his meal. My heart sinks, why am I such a silly girl? I stare at my supper and leave it untouched. I half listen to the endless chat, none of it registers, oh John, you silly man. Who cares about Bishop Boyd? I haven't seen Elizabeth for days, I fancy she's down in the clinic, maybe she's doing her best to stay close to the deceased Boyd – who knows? I shall find out tomorrow and visit her if that is possible.

I sleep fitfully, I dream of John Betts and Bernie, they look so good together.

At breakfast the funeral goers are gathered like black pads, all looking as if their funeral suits have been resurrected from a long passed age.

John, is among them pretending not to notice me. I respond by talking earnestly about nothing at all to a new resident whose name escapes me. The men troupe out to their taxi and are gone. In my room I feel really miserable, John oh John, why have you gone to that funeral, we never go to funerals, if anybody goes its McCann and co.

I dab my weepy eyes, God, I look awful, I spend the next half hour putting my face back on. When I believe I have reached a state of some composure, I set off to the Infirmary to visit Elizabeth. I have no idea what to expect, at least John Betts is pushed to the back of my mind, I wish I could push him back further but he always pushes himself forward. Don't, don't do that John, I see Lionel lurking in the background of my lurid mind.

I try to pull myself together, poor Elizabeth is obviously having a rough ride. I've thought about her a lot and tried to piece together possible reasons for her peculiar behaviour. She has always been shy, and apart from music and religion seems never to express herself at all. There must be something that she keeps locked up inside, I can only imagine it's something to do with her family and I suspect a deeply unhappy past. Anyway, she was kind to me when I first came here, and music has been our bond, so I must try my best. I find I am very nervous and apprehensive, I don't know why.

The young nurse who guards the entrance to the infirmary, looks about old enough to still be in school. Ms. Wainwright I am informed is in room four. She has been very unwell, the doctor has seen her every day and she is under a light sedative.

"Mrs Hayes-Bowen, please be aware that Ms Wainwright has been exhibiting unusual behaviour patterns, so please take care and if you feel there's any need for assistance please ring the red button."

She reads this warning rather like an air hostess, as if it were routine. I see a lack of compassion, it is too matter of fact, too impersonal, she is telling me that there's yet another unstable old biddy in room four. Who cares? Well, I do!

In room four, Elizabeth is sitting up in her bedside chair, she is tethered to a drip, her head lolls on her shoulder and dribbles of spit run down her chin. She does not move at all, she has no idea I'm in her room. Poor Elizabeth, has it come to this? A week or so ago we were arguing about this and that, looking forward to her cousin returning to play the piano, Oh,! Elizabeth my old friend what has happened to you?

I sit in the visitor's chair, I lean and gently as I can I wipe the spittle from her face. Her eyes open, she says nothing, but tears coarse down her ravaged face. I am overwhelmed with sadness, poor dear Elizabeth, she is drugged to pieces, whatever has happened to my sad friend.

"How are you my dear, it's Patricia here", I hold her sticky hands, and look into her deep sad eyes, there is someone there but far, far away. I feel as if I'm going to cry, I must not. Ms Wainwright is slowly and surely being put to death. I feel the freezing chill, I know they are not putting her down like a pet, but she stares into a void where we will all venture before too long.

I stay with Elizabeth for half an hour or more, I am deeply saddened, angry, that this is all they can do. Lock her up and fill her full of sedatives and watch her die. There is no doubt, that there's a much more complex picture behind the scene, but to me, my friend is being disposed of rather than cared for. So this is what it's like, I shiver as I walk back to my room, suddenly I turn to the lounge where I sit next to the fist conscious body I see. I want to talk, I want to share, I want my John back – now. I am afraid, maybe for the first time that soon, so soon, my time will end. How? That's the question. I feel a chill right through my bones. It's all John's fault, the bishop's funeral, they go to endless lengths to hide deaths from us and yet that wretched Bishop has somehow changed the rules. John has fallen for it, he behaved like an overgrown schoolboy, charging off with his chums to a funeral if you please. I am tormented, I want no more funerals, I want no more Elizabeth's, I want to be happy and not think about – you know what, certainly not funerals.

I do not recognise the lady I have joined in the lounge.

"Good afternoon, I don't believe we've met, my name is Patricia Hayes-Bowen."

The lady in question is dressed in a red cardigan and a silk shirt, she is somehow untidy, I can't quite make out what is wrong.

"My name's Betty, my husband is coming down soon. Have we met before?"

"No, we haven't met before, how long have you and your husband lived here?"

"Don, that's my husband, we live near Lyme Regis, do you know it?"

My heart sinks, another member of the Alzheimer's club. I tell myself to be kind, this lady is new here, or at least I think she is. My hands are shaking, "that's alright Betty, would you like a cup of tea?"

I wave at Alex, he smiles but walks out of the room. It seems Betty and I are to spend some time together.

"Just a week" says Betty, "just a week, I miss my Don, he passed six months ago, we lived near Lyme Regis, forty three years we'd been married, forty three years."

"Bless you Betty, you'll soon make friends here, there are lots of things to do. Do you like music?"

"Don liked music, he played the guitar, he loved his music, 'specially Dolly Parton, and all them"., she leans over me, "I think Don will be down in a minute." She has a red wrist band.

I can't do it, I really can't do it. "Look I must dash, bye Betty,"

I rush back to my empty room and sit exhausted and miserable. Sleep comes sweetly and wraps me in her warmth. I hope John comes home safe and sound. I dream of John watching me and Betty and Elizabeth all queuing up to get into our coffins, the line of coffins stretches on and on, Lionel beckons, and John waves good bye.

I wake with a start, it is only late afternoon, the spring sun is just below the top of my window, I am in my chair. I find it hard to move, there's a tapping on my door.

"Mrs. Hayes-Bowen, Ms. McCann would like to see you in her office, if that is possible/"

It's Alex, oh, heavens above what can it be? I
rouse myself, "Give me five minutes." I am in a
panic, I cannot remember what time it is.
Everything is confusion. I hastily wash my face
sit on the toilet and try hard to get things back
into focus. Does McCann want to see me?
Why? Who else will be there? Is it about
Elizabeth? Has John Betts been in an accident?

I take a deep breath, make up my face. I must
say putting on my face always makes me feel
more in control. Whatever is up, I can deal with
it. Can I? Don't think about it Patricia. I dither,
shall I put on different jewellery, yes, perhaps
this, perhaps that. I am exhausted, I sit down to
catch my breath.

There is a tapping at my door. It is Alex, "We
wondered when would be convenient Mrs.
Hayes Bowen, in fact Ms McCann is on her way
to see you is that OK?"

"Yes, yes, I have been asleep again, my nerves
are in shreds. Am I losing my mind?

I rush back to the bathroom its six thirty already, gracious it's time for dinner. Is my make up alright?

McCann has arrived, she looks immaculate as ever.

"Do sit down Patricia, may I?"

We both sit.

"It's not good news I'm afraid, I know you visited Ms. Wainwright this morning, and I know how friendly you have been. I'm afraid we've had to send her to the hospital, she's very unwell."

I recall Elizabeth's empty eyes, the runny nose and the dribbles. Oh dear I sigh. "I recall perfectly clearly, poor Elizabeth looked awful, do you know the problem?"

McCann puts her hand on mine, "I think dear Ms Wainwright is very ill, we should prepare for the worst."

Her duty done, McCann stands, pats my hand and leaves. I stare into space I don't know what to think. What a horrible couple of days, all my world is tumbling about me. Where is John Betts? It's time for supper, I go to my bathroom to check my makeup, I shall join the gentlemen for supper, I shall!

At supper there are none of my gentlemen, there are just a gaggle of ladies including Betty. I sit alone, I pray for some lucid company, John Betts please come home. There is a clatter and rumble of men's voices, in comes Brian and the Professor, and whatshisname. No John Betts.

"John is tired out he's gone up to his room, darling." Says Brian

"Long day," comments the Professor.

"Quite fun though", Giggles whatshisname.

Without any thought, I get up and leave, I don't know what to do. Shall I visit John? As if confidence deserts me, I wonder back to my room. John, John, oh how we need each other.

Tomorrow, Anna is coming with Dotty and we are to make our final decision about Abigail, I worry about John, will he come? I climb into bed, I can't sleep, our little Abi groups would not be the same without John. Why did I get so upset about the Bishop's funeral? Why did John seem to dislike me so much? It's all a muddle, I can't sleep, I don't sleep, John, John, John. I sleep and dream of Lionel pushing John into his coffin. I wake, the tears flow in a torrent. Nightmares, at my age. I feel so tired, I must sleep, the light begins to glimmer on my window. Will toady be a good day? Abi, we shall soon part, some young angel will make you sing and I shall just fade away.

Chapter 26.   John

My friend the Chaplain is very ill, he has been my good friend now for months, he doesn't bother me with the religious stuff but he certainly has his religious following. Liz Wainwright has always followed him about, and I've often wondered what a strange relationship this has been. In any event dear old Boyd has suddenly become very ill and I do my best to go see him every day. He was a brave soldier, even as a Chaplain, he told me how he crossed to meet local religious leaders in Northern Ireland, how he comforted the young soldiers and how he struggled himself with the cruelty and extremes of terrorism. Now his flock is small, strangely, not many of the Swallow House gang seem at all religious. I think Boyd used to be lucky to get half a dozen to his Sunday communions. However he was always available to everyone, even me. He is a lovely man. Boyd's flock was led by Liz Wainwright who to the end often hung about in the lockup waiting room. She seems more barmy that usual.

When it was announced that Boyd was to go to hospital, Wainwright, behaved even more oddly. She took great exception to me and my relationship with HB. I could not for the life of me understand her eccentricities. She went off the deep end when McCann announced the Bishop's passing. HB also got very ratty about the funeral and again I have no idea why. For the first time in a year I am on McCann's side, I know we usually don't dwell on friends passing on but nevertheless HB got really shirty about it. Tomos explained that ladies (la-ee-dees) of any age had diverging views from gentlemen. I see his point.

It is very hard to keep a sense of time, HB and I have been very close these last months, we go out on our treats and I'm very friendly with the delightful Doctor Dotty Knight, not to mention Anna Bryant who is an efficient as well as attractive lawyer. I have been so touched by HB and her almost religious relationship with her old violin. I must admit I was astonished when that gentleman from Bonham's came and started talking about such huge sums of money. I have never seen anyone as devoted as HB, she has almost spent all her spiritual reserves on the decisions about this wonderful violin. I really was knocked out by the sheer beauty of the thing, though I have never handled a violin, ever before.

Tomos has kept me on the straight and narrow, my shoulder is now almost back to normal. I must say, I have been feeling very well. The highlight of this year was David's visit, he was so lovely to HB, and I know this must have been a bit of a challenge for him. His old man cavorting with a new lady friend. However all that is behind me.

I went to Chichester with my friends to see Boyd off, it was with a heavy heart in more ways than one. HB seemed very cross about the whole venture, I do hope when I see her tomorrow that she has settled a bit. Tomorrow is an important day because we will (We HB, Dotty, Anna and me?) gather to support HB's decision on what happens to Abi. I do hope that we will be friends again, I know whatever decision she makes it will be hard for her and I want to be able to comfort her.

When we arrive back from Chichester its quite late, I am very, very tired. Dear old Tomos pours me a generous tot of Scotch, I am torn about how to make up with HB. I discuss this with Tomos as he helps me get my boot off.

"No Good, hiding, must go say hello lovely la-aa-dee, glad to see you, sorry we are cross with each other, all finish, kiss, make up. No problem, but first you need good rest. I get tablets." I was asleep before I could swallow my tablets.

Margaret and Johanna are as one, 'You must make up with HB, you are a silly boy. No place to fight about funerals, be kind, do your best.'

I have no difference with the advice, I am awake very early, the grandness of Boyd's funeral with Bishops and padres in their finery still vivid in my mind.. We old codgers at the back of the Cathedral, all looked forward to a beer on the way home. What were we doing there? We all avoid the subject, people come and people go, this is the first funeral I've been to in years. Geoff seemed entirely distracted whilst Brian typically wept throughout the ceremony. We were all relieved on the way home, we stopped at a pub and had a couple of beers and a rather ordinary pub supper of pie and chips. But still I enjoyed it. None of us mentioned Boyd except to toast his onward journey, whatever that meant. Anyway, it was long day, I am not sure if I spent it well or not, dear old Boyd would have liked to see us there but I think on the whole it was a long way to go for a couple of beers and that dreadful supper.

Still it's another day, an important one too, I must do as Margaret and Johanna tell me and make sure all is well with HB. I think I see her point about funerals, best left alone really.

"Good morning Mr John," Tomos sticks his head round the door. "It is nice morning and I think big day for HB violin, no?"

Tomos administers my daily intake of medication, helps me out of bed and then we tussle our way to the bathroom. As always I tell him to "bugger off", as always he does not.

"Today, I think meeting at eleven o clock, I think you put blazer and slacks change after breakfast, you must see HB and be sure of yourself, you see."

"Tomos, I get your drift but I must say I would have put it more clearly." My mild sarcasm zooms over Tomos' head.

"You must be having breakfast with HB, so nine o' clock sharp Mr John."

He's quite right, I dress carefully, Tomos helps with my boot, and I am ready to go at quarter to nine, shall I stay or shall I go. I am feeling quite nervous. Will HB tell me to bugger off? I know there was no reason for our spat, but I do remember how difficult women can be even Johanna.

In the dining room there are three tables to choose from, the boys, Brian and Geoff and Whatshisname or a one with a lady I do not know, and an empty table. I skulk about at the back of the room pretending to look at the morning papers. One table remains empty, shall I sit at it? Will HB come down at the right time, what if I sit there and one of the new ladies comes down before HB?

HB enters she looks round, sees me and beckons ever so subtly at the empty table, in unseemly haste I speed toward her, tripping as I do, and nearly falling over my walking stick. I lean on the table where now two ladies are sitting and two teacups crash to the floor. 'Fuck it! I am making a complete mess of this. After profuse apologies and sundry carers running about, I eventually reach HB who now has another lady sitting with her. Damn!

"Good morning ladies, may I join you?"

"By all means do," says HB, "Quite an entrance if I might say so." She smiles, but it a smile of condescension. " this is Betty, this is Mr .John Betts."

Betty barely looks up from her teacup, she mutters something I know not what.

"I hope you are well, Madame", I nod to Betty.

"My husband will be down soon, we slept well last night, did you two?"

"You must excuse Betty, but Don will not be down this side of eternity." Remarks HB.

I am confused, who is this Betty, I must say the idea of sleeping with HB is quite appealing, however I dismiss the idea almost instantly. HB looks a little tired, I hope she's happy that our tiff is over, however I am by no means certain. I am unsure what to say, Betty rambles under her breath.

"My dear John," HB puts her hand on mine, I instantly feel the electricity, instantly my spirit soars. "I hope you are going to come to the 'Abi' meeting, I need your support. Today's the day for me to say goodbye to her, I need all the support I can get." She sees me eying Betty, "don't fret about Betty she' not in our world, at least most of the time."

"HB, of course I'll be there, you know I wouldn't be anywhere else by choice." I squeeze her hand.

"Good, Ana is coming, so is Dotty and a person form the Instrument Trust. I hope I can keep up with Ana and all that business about trusts and things. Dear John, I shall depend on you and Dotty as usual."

"Dear HB, you are the loveliest of ladies, and I know how tough this is going to be for you , but I think we've done all the research and explored all your options, and as you said , Abi will sing again in some young angel's hands."

We smile at each other, Betty still talks of 'Don' her long dead husband coming down for breakfast. Then she says something shocking, "Do you like sex still? Don is always pestering me, but I'm not all that keen. What do you think? do you two fuck often?"

HB, I can see is shocked to the core. She straightens up, "I must go to my room, I hope you and Don have a good day, excuse me."

I am still sitting there with my mouth wide open. I see Brian sniggering on the lads' table. "You must forgive me, dear lady, I must retire." I hobble away at the best speed I can muster. I hope she hasn't upset HB too much, oh dear, what a turn up.

The meeting assembles on time, Dr Dotty, Ana, and I sit, there is no sign of HB. We wait and at seven minutes past the hour HB makes her entrance with 'Abi' and her other bow case, carried by Alex. She looks absolutely lovely, she is in her blue dress and jacket with a beautiful brooch of a music clef in diamonds. Her hairs is silver and swept back beautifully, to show off her glorious diamond ear rings.

As always her make up is perfect, but I see tiny signs of sadness, however she hold herself straight as if she were about to go on stage. I admire her, no I love her. She is at once beautiful and noble, petite and strong, immaculate and human. How could I not love her?

Ana is the first to react, she takes 'Abi' and lays her down gently, then she hugs HB. Dotty follows suit, and I am hopelessly rooted to my

314

chair. I struggle to my feet and HB and I do a double hand hold and just look into out tearful eyes.

After around half an hour of Ana going through the trust agreement, we all signed as witnesses and waited anxiously for the trust representatives who arrived about fifteen minutes late. However Messrs Gregorich and Flittoff were so charming as to be almost unreal. Their most important announcement was that 'Abi' would be lent to a young violinist of considerable accomplishment. Born in Russia to musical parents, Maria Sashanova began playing the violin aged four. Moving to England in 2001 after her father was appointed a principal with the London Symphony Orchestra, she began studies at the Yehudi Menuhin School (where her mother now teaches violin). In 2006 Maria Sachanova won the London Symphony Orchestra Music Scholarship and became a BBC New Generation Artist. Her first CD was the complete violin works of Karl Amadeus Hartmann in 2017, which was followed by the two violin concertos of Nikolai Roslavets in 2018. With regular recital partner Cédric Tiberghien and in solo and chamber music, Maria has appeared at venues including the Wigmore Hall, Concertgebouw, Mozarteum, Musikverein and Carnegie Hall. Performing a wide range of repertoire extending from baroque to contemporary works, Sashanova is widely celebrated for her wildly imaginative playing, combining unleashed energy and historical awareness. She has also been the recipient of a number of awards including the Royal Philharmonic Society Young Artist Award 2020, Borletti- Buitoni Trust and a Classical BRIT.

This amazing CV had HB in tears. Moreover we were informed that if the trust completed the loan agreement Ms. Sashanova would be happy to invite HB and a her friends to a concert in London or Bournemouth which would be dedicated to Patricia Hayes (no mention of Bowen). Dates would also be arranged for Maria

Sashanova to visit Swallow House to meet HB as soon as her schedule would allow it.

It would be fair to say that all of us, especially HB were over the moon. When the foundation folk left after lunch, it was as if a great weight had been moved from HB's shoulders. We were all excited and weary, we had sparkling wine with lunch and I am certainly fit to have a nap. Anna makes her farewell with Dotty and HB and I were left not quite staggering from the board room. I must say McCann had done us proud and for once did not interfere in the proceedings.

Back at HB's rooms, I hold HB and she sinks into my arms, I feel her giving me her life and love. "Come John, let's nap together," only snag is we have to embrace on her couch as the bed is a single hospital affair with steel safety bars. We sit together on her settee and we kiss, gently, then curled up in each other's arms we sleep.

Chapter 27

Summer tip toes over Swallow House, the garden looks lovely, still unkempt, but beautiful despite that. HB and I spend hours sitting outside even when the skies are grey, we never run out of things to talk about, we are even content to sit and hold hands and say nothing at all.

It is two months since Abi was given on perpetual loan to the Trust and we have heard this very morning that Ms Sashanova will be coming to see us next week. She will be happy to play a short concert and will be accompanied by a piano playing partner. We do not know who this will be.

When we learn of the impending event, HB is up and off like a whippet, she barges into McCann's office insisting our boudoir grand piano is tuned without delay. HB, at her most forceful, insists it was done as soon as possible and at her, HB's own expense. McCann, I understand acceded to HB's assault, being mindful of battles which can be won or not.

We are both beside ourselves with excitement, HB comes alive, years, seem to be shed as if by magic. She truly looks lovelier than ever I had seen her. I can hardly believe that life could be so good, we are both full of energy and sheer joy. So this is what love is about, no matter what our age, no matter where we are, and no matter who we are. In all my eighty five years I had never felt more alive. We are about to share in something we both fervently love. It is a silk chain that binds us, it envelopes us in a shared passion.

There is a mighty palaver about the piano tuner, McCann has reported back this afternoon that there is not a piano tuner to be found anywhere that can turn up before next Wednesday. HB, uncharacteristically immediately takes charge. "John, we must ring Dotty and Anna right away, we have to find a tuner or the whole visit will be let down. John, John, what are we to do."

"Steady down my dear, the piano seems fine to me, let's go see what you think, you have a very fine ear still, so don't panic."

In the conservatory I heard HB play for the first time, she is not spectacular, she chooses some simple pieces, but even to my ear I can sense her musicality. To me the piano sounds fine. HB however is less than satisfied.

"It's out, it's out, oh John it's not bad but there are lots of issues albeit minor ones." She wrings her hands, "John, before you say anything, please understand I will not allow this poor girl to play Abi with an out of tune piano, please don't say another word."

I know when I am beaten, so I keep my lip buttoned. Anna came up with a tuner the following morning and we all sigh with relief, he can come on Saturday and will charge the earth. HB is unconcerned, as long as he turns up.

I am aware that if you are in a bubble you cannot see it, but in a bubble we are. Time flies, even our little naps together seem shorter. We wake trying to burn the time between us and the recital. The piano tuner does turn up, he does know what he's doing much to HB's delight. He is a lovely man who is blind, he's been driven here by his daughter, they are both an absolute delight.

HB gives us a sample of Fur Elise and a little Mozart and announces she is delighted. She then insists the piano is locked.

"Do you think that's necessary HB? Frankly I don't know if McCann will find the key."

HB is positive, the key is unearthed and the piano locked. HB takes custody of the key, the whole thing HB makes into a dramatic event. I remain sceptical about the whole issue.

On Sunday HB is taken out for lunch by one of her DSA chums, I am surprisingly jealous, I skulk in my rooms. I miss Tomos who is having his day off. Tomos has been such a good friend to me, without him, I would never have recovered as well as I have done. When I next speak to David on Skype I must remember to make a provision for him in my will. Being alone through a long Sunday afternoon brings me to the provisions of my will. In the melancholy of my brief loneliness, I slide down easily toward the darkness of nothing. I make a note to mention Tomos when I next speak to David.

My sleep, is fitful, my insecurity floods back, what if HB were to be taken away, what will HB do when I am gone, my sleep is fitful, sometimes deep and dark.

Down in the dining room it is quite empty, Sunday is a day when relatives remember they have old Uncles, Aunts, and Mums and Dads fading away in Swallow House. It's very much like my old school days when we had leave outs, I used to hate them because my Mum cold seldom come and see me.

"Hello darling, are you all alone, well, well, poor you." Tweets Brian. He's not so gently taking the mickey.

"Hello, you old perv, just the two of us for tea"

In two minutes we are chatting about everything under the sun, including HB, everyone has long since got used to us as a couple. I am warmed by the subject.

"I do hope we can all come on Wednesday, to the recital I mean, everybody's talking about it."

"Up to HB old boy, but I'm sure everyone will be welcome."

On Monday HB receives a note from the instrument Trust, outlining what time Ms Sashapova will arrive, with some options for Ms Patricia Hayes to choose from. The recital will be informal. There will be a senior member of the trust, Ms Sashapova's Manager, her accompanist, as well as the young violinist.

HB is now so excited, she's in a whirl of uncontrolled enthusiasm. She has made McCann's life quite miserable, with umpteen requests from seating plans, to luncheon requirements, and guest list, her energy is astonishing.

Wednesday dawns, I am awake very early, before Tomos has turned up. That early! I cannot wait to see HB, today is a big day, a big day in my eighty five year life. I know too, that's it's a bigger day for HB. I pray immediately that nothing will go wrong and then of course I imagine everything that can go wrong.

By the time Tomos turns up, I am up and showered and half dressed. "Mr John, what you do so early? Too excited, be careful you have heart attack."

"Don't talk bollocks Tomos, today is going to be a great day."

"Look you shave very bad, Mr John you must take time."

He's right of course, but it's not too late and I'm already in a state of high excitement. It's still only eight o'clock, breakfast won't start till nine. I look out of the window it's a nice day, I think I will walk in the garden before breakfast.

"Right, Tomos, let's walk in the garden, it's a nice day."

"Mr John you are a crazy man, but OK if you want."

My hope of meeting HB in the garden is dashed there is only one lady who I don't know, she bids me good morning and "Good luck with the recital."

Wow! Everybody is aware and looking forward to this afternoon. It does nothing to calm my nerves. Our walk in the garden is shortened by the demands of my nervous digestion. Back to the room, then and Tomos supervises my fashion selection, at least for breakfast. It's nearly nine o clock time for an entry to the dining room.

Eventually HB makes an entrance, she looks absolutely marvellous, so much younger than her age. She joins me at the table, pecks me on the cheek, brazenly in front of everyone. I'm not sure I can blush anymore I just hope nobody was watching. I think I hope nobody was watching, on the other hand I feel rather pleased, I hope they were watching. HB has reams of paper, and despite my effort to pour the tea, rather pushes them in front of me.

"Tea dear," I ask.

"Never mind the tea, I don't think we included the piano page turner for lunch, oh dear what shall we do?"

"Put another chair at the lunch table." I say helpfully.

"Oh, you men! "

"Tea Dear?"

I can see she is tetchy, excited and nervous, all at once. "Relax my dear, all will be well I'm sure of it."

"How do you know, what if the page turner doesn't show up?"

"Look, dear HB, your sudden preoccupation with a page turner, what's it all about?"

"Last night in bed, I thought the Beethoven sonata will need a page turner, I just hope they have one in the party."

I'm not entirely sure what a page turner does, so I keep my counsel.

After a non-breakfast, just one piece of toast and nothing for HB, I am dragged into the conservatory where we go round each name place on the chairs. There is no chair for the page turner, Tomos who always follows at a distance is hailed and a chair from the back of the room is placed very precisely to the left of the piano stool. HB looks pleased.

"There she says, 'perfect'" and without looking back makes her way to the Board room where lunch will be served before the recital. The same issue arises about the bloody page turner, I just shove in a chair between Dr Knight and me. Who cares for goodness sake?

"I hope the caterers will be able to handle an extra plate" It's that page turner again, my patience is wearing thin, time for me to withdraw.

Twelve fifteen and a large limo arrives dead on time. McCann dressed to the nines is waiting with HB and Anna at the main entrance. I am not at all sure where I should stand or sit or perhaps disappear altogether. We are all to attend pre-lunch refreshment in McCann's office. There is quite a large posse of people. I crane my neck to catch a glimpse of Maria

Sashapova. She is not tall, she has a dark head of hair, not very tidily assembled. She is not glamorous at all. Rather a long and 'bony' face, her nose predominates. She wearing trousers and a blouse with a scarf wrapped about her neck. I think she looks like a very ordinary girl indeed. I think I'm disappointed.

Then, there comes a really pretty young lady, and another, am I mistaken? Who are all these people?

I think I recognise Mr Gregorich from the Trust, there's another young man casually dressed, the two pretty girls, a man who carries the violin, just too many to take in. I am suddenly very tired, I want to go and lay down, but of course I can't. I hope HB is feeling better than me.

HB passes me without a nod, she's deep in conversation with the plain Sashapova, everyone else trails behind, and even McCann doesn't seem to know her place.

All the wine remains unopened and as far as I can see no one seems particularly interested in the lovely salad luncheon either. HB is the centre of attention, I am left to make conversation with the dreaded McCann. McCann does her best to humour me, but I must say the whole thing so far is a disappointment.

The lunch stutters to a close. There is, I gather, a half hour delay while the conservatory is finally ready and the ladies have done what ladies do. I am stuck with the nice but boring Gregorich from the instrument trust and McCann. We, with Anna and Dotty chat over coffee. Suddenly the door bursts open and it is HB looking exceedingly anguished. "The key, the key to the piano, its locked!"

The look on her face is one of sheer panic, her 'composed centre of attention', 'aren't I wonderful' radiance seemed to have disassembled in a trice. I am shocked she looks as if the curtain has gone up to reveal a stressed old lady. Oh! My lovely HB, what have you done?

McCann is the first to react, she I must say immediately imposes an air of calm. "Mrs Hayes Bowen, you had the key after the tuner came, just relax and remember what you did with the key after that."

HB's expression hardly changes, she's like a rabbit caught in the headlights. It dawns on me that she has quite forgotten all about the key, the tuner, she stares blankly, I can see her trying her best to return from the land of 'nothing' to be back with us.

McCann, stands and embraces HB, I am a bit taken aback, surely I should be doing something.

"Relax, Patricia, relax, just think now, when did the piano tuner come?"

HB stares ahead, eyes unblinking. She seems in a trance. Dr. Dotty puts her arms round HB, "it will be alright, Patricia, alright." They lead her to a chair, where she sits, bereft, confused and sad.

I remember, the bloody key, the goddamn page turner. "I know where the key is" I say somewhat triumphantly.

They all turn and stare at me. Dotty and I hare off to PH's room with the master door key from McCann, 'she put the key in her make-up bag. I remember distinctly, let's hope we can find the bag and the key. Secretly I fume, I had an inkling that this might be all too much for HB.

We scramble into HB's rooms and Dotty goes straight to the bathroom. She emerges almost immediately key in hand, She kisses me on the cheek, "Lovely boy, John and we both rush as best we can back to the expectant company. HB still looks shocked and lost. Dotty waves the key and the piano is prepared. Everyone is now concerned about HB, but as soon as the piano accompanist strikes up, it's as if HB emerges from her nothingness. She smiles, yes, yes of course everything is in order.

HB is ushered to the ladies room by Dr Dotty, and we all assemble in the conservatory. Ms Sachapova really looks upset and concerned, but the rest of the crew pianist, page turner, manager and electrician/recording bloke carry on as professionals. Eventually, HB and Dotty return, HB is back to her poised self, we are all mightily relieved.

Ms Sachapova rushes over when HB is sat down twixt me and Dotty, she hold the violin for HB to caress. "I hope I can play for you, Ms. Hayes, this is the most beautiful violin, I pray I can do it justice. "

Then she stepped back, tunes the violin, and plays. It was a torrent from Heaven, first unaccompanied and then accompanied by the piano. I felt HB beside me shiver and sob as the waves of wonderful sound enveloped her. After forty minutes or so, Ms Shasapova played Franz

Schubert's arrangement of 'Ave Maria' beautifully accompanies on the piano. I swear that in all my like I have heard nothing more beautiful.

At the end there was a stunned silence, HB rose to her feet and embraced Ms Sachanova. "You are so lovely," She held the violist's hand and turned to us and said, "Abi has gone home, and what a wonderful home it will be." We all came to, as it were, and clapped with almost superhuman enthusiasm.

The visiting party departed after tea and more congratulations to the musicians, Mr Gregorich promised to keep in touch and arrange a public concert during which once more the gift of Abi would be celebrated.

It is evening by the time we all settled down, I feel absolutely exhausted. Still very much in my mind is HB's welfare, I was really alarmed over the piano key affair. Dr Dotty I know shares my anxiety. Despite my exhaustion, I take HB aside and tell her to rest, she is still excited.

"John, don't fuss, it has been the most wonderful day, what a wonderful recital."

Her eyes still sparkle as if this earlier episode with the key had never been. Dotty Knight, stays for tea, she winks at me as I take my leave. I raise my eyebrows in conspiratorial fashion, we both know HB has given her all and I will trust Dotty to come up with a plan, a care plan for HB, because as surely as the sun rises, there will be a reaction.

Chapter 28

HB has seen her vision achieved, she is almost in a state of shock, as if she has been given everything she has ever wanted. She is content for us to sit in her room and listen over and over again the Sharapova recital.

She misses Abi, she constantly looks at the wardrobe that has been Abi's home for the last many years. I think she is conflicted, giving Abi to the Foundation, was like giving away her second child. She does not confess her loss, she merely plays the disc over and over.

I share with Dr Knight my misgivings about what I see as HB's change of personality, it is not that she is not affectionate, she is, perhaps a little more distant. She is haunted by the sound of Abi being played so beautifully by Shasapova. Is she jealous? Of youth, of the music she will never play, of her long lost Bernie and Tim, she has turned in on herself. I feel a little locked out. I hate this change, we are growing not old but very old. It seems our ability to absorb emotion is so limited. Me, I sleep a lot, I hope a lot, I wait a lot for HB to ring or Dotty to call for our outings. Waiting, is very close to nothing and I have always hated that.

Summer passes, our lives are still close, I still long to spend time with HB, she is still sweet but her eyes are not as bright as they were.

It is September, a letter arrives it is from the Foundation, we HB and I, are invited to a performance of the Bournemouth Symphony Orchestra in Bristol. Top of the bill will be Ms Sharapova, playing Sibelius' violin concerto. There is immediate mayhem, once more HB wakes from her emotional slumber, we are agog with excitement.   Dr Dotty and Anna, are thrilled, the itinerary includes a chauffeur driven limo to Bristol, a five star hotel room for two, a pre- concert reception by the Orchestra sponsors and a dinner after the concert with the conductor, soloist and orchestra leaders etc..

The date is six weeks ahead. The first issue is who will share a room with HB. I am keenness itself, but the ladies insist that their will be enough excitement, and that we should all have single rooms with Tomos in attendance. Much to my disappointment this what we settle on. The six weeks are a maelstrom of arrangements and rearrangements. HB rushes off with Dotty to buy clothes for the occasion, Tomos digs out my old dinner jacket, I wonder if I can tie my bow tie like I used to. It's an amazing puzzle, Tomos and I spend hours practising until I just about get it right. Tomos and I fight about a clip on tie as opposed to tying my own, you simply can't trust these Albanians!

My lovely girls Margaret and Johanna, counsel me each dawn, take your time they say. Be patient they say, be kind to HB because she will find the whole thing extremely emotional. 'Be there John' 'be there for her' they tell me.

Adding to the excitement is an impending visit from my son and his lovely wife Shanta, it is almost too much to take in, I find myself panicking. Then one week to go, and I feel like death. I am coughing, and snorting like a pig. The doctor comes Dotty closely behind and they administer what they feel will give me a chance to get to Bristol. With five days to go the prospects look grim. HB is not allowed to visit me in case she catches whatever I've got. I feel very low, Tomos is cheerful as always, and encourages Mr John, usually preceded by an effing commentary on my ailments. I cough effing back at him.

Three days to go and I am out of bed, still feeling pretty rough, my gammy leg always plays up when I am off colour. I am still not allowed to speak to HB face to face. Then the doctor relents with two days to go and I receive

HB in rooms. She looks so pretty, she is full of beans. She exercises no restraint at all and hugs me, "John, I've missed you, you must come on Saturday, you must!"

"My darling I will do my best, even if it kills me! Isn't that how we all started?" She hugs me once more,

"You must, you must!" She sounds about twenty years younger than when we last met. She is the best medicine I've received and I certainly feel much better.

As Tomos would say, "Fuck it, we'll go to Bristol." And go we do.

Confusion is something never far away. If it were not for Tomos this odyssey would almost certainly not come about. Tomos, takes infinite care on packing for the Bristol trip, it will be the first time I have spent outside Swallow House for ever. I am quite nervous, the outside world, full of bullies and young thugs is a daunting place. Memories of the youngsters on the bus, of Dave and Tarry all come flooding back. I have become a delicate old fossil, I know it and I am ashamed of it. As we pack ready for our trip to Bristol I am filled with fear and foreboding. This morning my lovely wives all chirped in with encouragement, especially about looking after HB. However by the looks of things HB may well have to look after me. I am very aware perhaps for the first time that Swallow House has become my bastion against a fading world. If it were not for HB, I'd be back to Geoff and his peaceful pill.

My nerves are on edge, HB is to the contrary like a demented butterfly. She hums these tunes, even complex baroque tunes which I find at first pleasant and then aggravating. By the time we bundle into the limousine, I am exhausted. HB continues to hum Sibelius or whatever. Dr Dotty and Anna are the supporting cast with Tomos acting as my batman beside the driver. I hope I'm the only one who can hear him effing under his breath.

One of the major issues is pee stops, both HB and I need relief at regular intervals, so the limousine stops at prechosen hostelries on an hourly basis. This has all been planned by our lovely doctor Dotty. I keep on trying to act the suave Lothario and at least pay for a coffee, but each time I am rebuffed – everything has been taken care of by the sponsor of this evening's concert.

After our second stop I notice that HB has stopped humming, she has become quiet. Dotty has noticed and gently prompts HB with comforting comments and questions. Once more I see nothing descend and HB withdraws into a waking sleep. She stares ahead, aware but not aware. All of us become very uncomfortable. She sleeps, we make her comfortable on my shoulder, I am afraid that my lovely HB is unwell. The country side passes, the drizzle falls, and HB sleeps. Please God let's get through this day.

We arrive at our Hotel as it transpires a little early. The rooms are not ready. Tomos rants under his breath, even Dotty is showing signs of strain and we all troop to the lounge where the marketing manager of tonight's sponsor greets us with feigned enthusiasm. I can't help but notice how his face drops when he sees me and HB, two not so golden oldies stagger into the lounge. We have to wait, and Mr Watkins, the marketing manager, fusses and has really no idea what to do. He whispers to the ladies, and looks furtively at HB and I as if one of us is about to do something awful, like faint or die or something. I feel he may not be too wide of the mark. I really do feel very tired and I know HB feels the same. She has at least recovered from her catalepsy in the car and seems aware of what's going on. She is starting to hum again. It occurs to me that tonight she may hum through the concert which will drive me mad.

At last we are shown to our rooms, Tomos and I go one direction and the ladies the other. The time table is demanding, cocktails in the preconcert reception, the concert itself, then dinner with assorted celebrities. Mr Watkins briefs us on who's who' but I instantly forget. I see HB concentrate, but she's fighting a losing battle.

Tomos bundles me into bed, we have three hours of much needed rest. The bed is very comfortable, sleep comes quickly and deeply. Tomos gently wakes me it is five o clock, time to dress.

"Come, Mr John, we must make you smart guy, you big celebrity tonight, bow tie all, all."

Bless Tomos what would I do without him. I really care for him, he's not just my batman, he's my friend, he really cares for me. I feel I can trust him with everything from my underpants to my bank account, the guy is an absolute Godsend.

We assemble at six, HB looks like some Hollywood star, fabulously dressed in a pale blue evening gown, at her throat a very beautiful necklace I have never seen before. Her hair is sculpted beautifully showing her firm silver hair above two diamond and pearl earrings. She takes my breath away. Dr Dotty and Anna are none too shabby either both ladies in their most elegant attire. As Tomos and I enter Anna is kind enough to give a gentle wolf whistle, which I know is just to boost my flagging confidence.

The reception was lovely and I am very much the spectator. Anna becomes my escort, whilst Dotty sticks to HB who is feted by all and sundry. Anna watches me like a hawk and I am allowed just one glass of champagne. Into the concert we go with HB and I in the best seats alongside the sponsors and their principal guests. I regret to say I am so tired I have to fight not to sleep. The programme is all about Sibelius and the highlight is his violin concerto played by none other than Maria Shasapova. The whole thig is a huge success. At the end of the violin concerto Ms Shasapova hailed HB who was ushered to her feet. To thunderous applause HB acknowledged her accolade and we all feel very proud of her. I am ashamed to say that Anna has to nudge me awake during the performance of Sibelius' fifth symphony. Apparently I'd been snoring.

The post-concert dinner was also a very fancy affair, HB still the toast of the town. I am dismayed when we are allocated separate tables, HB with the soloist and conductor and me with one of the sponsors and the leader of the orchestra. It all passes in a blur. HB looks blissful in the centre of attention. I believe I am jealous. Anna is lovely and I do my best to talk of violins and music about which I know little.

Our party leaves the dinner somewhat the worse for wear. Certainly I have drunk too much Merlot, however HB still seems to on cloud 9. I try my best to tell her how lovely everything has been, but I find myself incoherent and mildly ill tempered. By God, I don't think I've ever been so tired. I kiss HB goodnight, and withdraw to my room with a certain sense of relief. Tomos, that's who I want to see. He'll help me into bed, and then I can sleep. Am I too old to love, actually I think I'm too tired to think about it. Orpheus opens his arms, it's been a lovely day, HB is fulfilled, where am I?

We return the following morning, HB still flying on the wings of her fame. I feel a little underwhelmed, my chill seems to be returning. Dr Dotty is as always solicitous, the conversation slows and soon everyone is asleep except Tomos and the driver.

HB and I we still care for each other. As winter comes we sit in our rooms and read if we can, or listen to music. I have noticed that HB is different, she has changed. She is more distracted somehow. She follows Ms Shasapova's career with a microscope, she receives monthly reports from Shasapova's PR team, she listens to the classical radio stations and has become obsessed with the player and her beloved Abi. Sometimes I find it hard to be so mono minded. However she is still my love, she is still my gentle friend, she still holds my hand and she still makes my world go round.

David and Shanta arrive in early December just before Christmas no doubt to shower me with gifts I don't need or for that matter want. Their kids are off somewhere, so we celebrate with an enormous party that even includes McCann. I'm so happy and proud, David is hosting this lovely luncheon for Dotty, Anna, our Trust lady, HB, McCann, and of course me. As always these December lunches have their sad ends.

There is a crash, we turn, HB is on the floor. I stand unmoving, trying to comprehend what has happened. Dotty is at her side, she lies there her skirt obscenely above her knee. David and Shanta rush to help, they pick her up, the light no longer shines, the mercurial musical nymph is gone, just like that, after lunch on a Thursday.

I am ushered away, but I know, I know, HB my muse, my handholding love is gone. Gone to talk to Margaret and Johanna. Gone and left me, once more I am abandoned, left to be a nuisance to David Shanta and their kids.

Tomos appears, he has tears in his eyes. I do not, I am alone, I am cold, I am unnecessary, I am all used up. I feel as if I'm standing on the station and the last train has gone. They crowd around me in a loose scrum of affection, they all avoid any reference to HB, my HB, I feel the tears come, I grieve once more.

For all her faults, McCann shows great sensitivity, she almost sees what I am thinking. Shanta as beautiful as ever and McCann smelling of roses as usual, take me, lead me back to the car. HB and all are still in the Pub, phones are ringing, there! I hear the siren of the approaching but useless ambulance. HB has gone, Tomos puts his arm around me relieving the fragrant McCann who whispers instructions to him, Shanta and Tomos take me back to Swallow House where we sit in McCann's office waiting hopelessly for news. I know the news. HB is dead, gone, ended. I cry and my daughter in law holds me gently as my tears roll down my decrepit face. Where to now?

In my rooms there is not quiet, the word has got round, Brian is the first to come his handkerchief already soaked with tears, then Geoff, his gaunt frame somehow sagging as if he too has lost a friend. Tomos presides over a whiskey drinking ceremony, only to be interrupted by David and Shanta who after some difficult introductions join us and we all toast the passing of my musical love. Chaos rains, of course, and as night falls and my guests depart, I have no idea what tomorrow will bring. Tomos who has been beside me since day break, pulls the cover over me and astonishingly kisses me lightly on my forehead.

"Thank you Tomos, now bugger off." He smiles and closes my bedroom door and the night closes in. My girls are there, all holding each other's hand, sleep, they say in chorus, sleep tomorrow will be another day

Chapter 29.

In Swallow House, another day starts, another resident has passed. Breakfast is served at nine to nine thirty as usual. Tomos is at my side very early, he is aware that I am for ever changed. We are silent, we do not josh about, we do not swop 'eff' words. I do not wish to go down to breakfast, I have much to do. I must comfort my children and let them see that HB' passing is just an ordinary matter of fact happening. I must conceal my grief. The last thing I want is their Christmas ruined so they have to look after me.

My mind is made up, HB's time was up and so is mine, no good bleating about it. Yes, I will miss HB dreadfully, but they mustn't know. Tomos knows, I know, I think the dreaded McCann knows, but I must be brave, I must pretend that HB was and is nothing to me.

Tomos has provided tea, and I sit in silence. The kids went to their hotel last night in a state of shock, when they return I must assure them of my strength and mental wellbeing. There's a knock on the door, it's McCann with Doctor whatshisname. She stands, perfectly dressed, perfectly composed as always.

"John, I'm very sorry to confirm that Patricia Hayes Bowen suffered a stroke yesterday and has not survived. John, I'm very sorry I know how fond of each other you were."

Silly bitch, of course I know HB has gone, she'd gone by the time she hit the floor. Anyway, I must be nice.

"Thank you Joan, you're very considerate, but I'm quite aware of HB's passing. Look its very awkward, with David here, we have to make sure that he knows I'm all right, I don't want him and his wife wrecking their Christmas, so please, please Joan, do the best you can my dear, and encourage them to go back to America and not worry about me. Of course they're upset, but I do not want to mess up their Christmas. Understood?"

"Yes, of course, but it will help if the doctor here takes a look at you and then we can reassure everyone that you are well, is that OK John?"

"I'm fine thank you but I'll pop down to the medical centre later if that's all right. Bloody mess, if you know what I mean. Not that I mean HB did anything untoward, it's just that David and Shanta are here."

I feel very tired, I sit, Tomos offers tea, McCann, as always avoids any in depth conversation and takes her leave.

Brian, then Geoff all pop in, they all have nothing to say except they're sorry, whatever that means. Nobody really gives a damn. This is the end of the line, I know it, they know it, we know it. Is it sad? Yes it is, my HB is no more, the pretty face, the neat hair the sweet and lovely hands. Her wonderful musicality, her sweet kindness, her wonderful friends, all gone!

What's the bloody point of it all? I am falling
hopelessly into nothing. Strangely, that's OK,
the real problem lies with taking other people
with me. How can I uncouple the love I have for
David and his lovely brood? There hangs the
rub!

Time passes, I've been up and about for ages.
Even my visit to the medical centre proved a
non-event. It seems I remain in the rudest health.

David and Shanta arrive by late morning, there
is a bleakness in the room. They don't know
what to say, and I have not very much to say.
It's like charades without the humour.

David announces, supported by the nodding and
beautiful Shanta that the whole family will come
and spend Christmas in England. "The kid's
will love it."

 No they bloody won't, it's the daftest idea I've
heard in a while. Everything is shambolic,
David has postponed his flight back to the US,

I'm not sure what I should be doing; crying or playing the 'I don't care card'.

Dr, Dorothy Wright and her husband appear, my room is like a fair, nowhere left to sit. They are all trying to be kind and I am absolutely non-plussed. No idea what to do or what to say. To make things worse Dotty, David and Shanta hustle into little whispering cliques, they must think I'm a useless old fart. I know they have no idea what to do either, it's an absolute buffer crunch, all our worlds seem to be reduced to chaos. HB would be really annoyed if she knew what chaos she's wrought.

I have decided to pack it all in, this shambles of everyone trying to tread on eggshells, HB is dead, gone, buggered off, I know she's say something more genteel like 'passed away' but it's all the same in the end. I am getting tired, it is Tomos who eventually gently steers the crowd out, to conspire somewhere else. I am greatly relieved. Tomos administers a large midday whiskey, how salving it is. Warm honey and nettles comfort me, Scotch was never better.

Switching off is impossible, David and Shanta refuse to leave, they visit every day. We wait for HB's funeral which is many days away. I play the cool hand of someone who doesn't care, I invite Geoff and co to interrupt David's visits, I am trying my utmost to push David and Shanta away. They are so beautiful, so kind, this is the hardest thing I've ever tried to do. Both David and Shanta look as if they've aged ten years. Not only did they experience HB's dramatic end, they've seen their father behave like a self-centred prick ever since.

"The kids will be missing you. Time you went, don't worry about me, you must get home." My constant witter. They stare back and argue hopelessly for me to go with them.

At last it's time to cremate my old love, it is as if the play is coming to an end. At last, I have persuaded my lovely son and his wife to get back to their children. It is a great weight off my mind. I can be softer now, wipe my tears in public, hold the lovely Shanta's hand, lean on Dr Dotty.

I never liked funerals and HB's was no exception. The Eulogy was shared between Dotty and the President of the DSA. It was all beautiful, even the music, but not as beautiful as my HB. As I slept at last, the three of my loves all held me, HB is at home, Margaret and Johanna hold her in their friendly embrace. "Soon John, soon." They say in chorus.

'Farewell', an easy word to say. But now I have to brave farewell to David and Shanta, whose visit started so brightly and is ending in such shadow. Even the clouds gather round Swallow House, swirling with cold dark misery, everyone knows today will be the last time I will ever hold my boy and his lovely wife. Today in the greyness of a cold December noon, I will release them to their lives without me. They will fly away for me to live out my miserable days as best I can. How painful will this last hug be? How brave will we all be? I know David is all in pieces, how I've always loved him, how I've rejoiced in his success, how I shall miss him for ever. Be brave John Betts, now at the last you must be brave

McCann, says good bye, and leaves us to coffee after a pleasant lunch, not that I have eaten anything. It has been an hour of false jollity, of superficial chit chat, about US houses and healthcare, about the grandkids.

"Goodbye David and Mrs Betts, come on Tomos, let's leave John and his family to say their goodbyes." She gets up her suit as always immaculate her makeup perfect, so perfectly organised.

"No, Tomos, stay, I'll need you to help me when they've gone." Tomos slinks to the back of the room and offers, "I be outside Mr John."

"Well Dad, you sure you won't come with us?"

"David, we've been through all that I'm quite happy and settled here, Off you go now and the give the kids a hug from me." We hug a second too long, the tears and just about under control.

"Shanta, look after him won't you." She envelops me in great hug, "Be sure I will," she says, I feel her tears run down the side of my face.

"Get out of here, have a great Christmas, we'll skype as soon as you get home! Tomos! – let's get back to the room."

The winter is wet, wet, wet, the rain knows no end. In Swallow House, a quiet descends, we few gentlemen who are still in touch with reality, meet seldom despite the proximity of our quarters. We seldom make breakfast as a group, The Professor has been unwell for weeks. His room out of bounds because of a flu contagion. Brian has suddenly got old, his handkerchief flies less brightly, his voice quiet almost a whisper now. Amongst the ladies, I barely recognise anyone any more.

Chapter 30

The worst thing of all, Tomos has gone, expelled by some civil servant as an interloper, an unqualified immigrant who the Government say is not wanted. I am heart broken, how can they do this? Do they not know that Tomos has the heart of a lion and the kindest soul there has ever been. The worst thing was that in February he just disappeared, another young man appeared. The bastards knew, they just kicked Tomos out. McCann said it couldn't be helped and that Winston, that's his name would be the perfect carer for me. Well, he is not. He knows nothing, he is a humourless halfwit, a bumbling idiot who I do not like. I fumed and spat and shouted but it did no good.

Winston is now firmly of the opinion that I am a geriatric mess, intemperate, occasionally incontinent, and reliant on alcohol. Fuck him! My life has become a constant struggle, Winston needs the sack, out, out, out he must go. I will manage on my own. Winston is a useless piece of crap, he can't even manage the Skype thing, absolutely fucking useless.

I have battled with McCann, she just humours me, the bitch. For ever the school matron.

It has stopped raining, I want to go into the garden, but I can no longer walk, at least not easily. The useless Winston, tries to keep me incarcerated in my room. I'll show him, I wait till he's on his break, he has about ten a day, the lazy bugger. As I close my door behind me I reach for the hand rail, I miss and before I know it I'm on the floor. I lie there, my leg hurts, my hand hurts, I refuse to press my panic button. Sod them all, I will lay here and blame Winston, that will show them!

Winston finds me and he kicks me, he kicked me in my side. He pretends he didn't but he did. He pulls me roughly to my feet, I see the loathing in his eyes. We stare at each other, he's a vindictive little shit, I shall get him, I'm not sure how, but I'll get him.

My war with Winston continues. Winston is Scottish, comes from Glasgow, he is slight in stature and looks feral to me. He is an unpleasant person altogether, it is not simply that I compare him to Tomos. This guy does not like me. He does not like old people at all. I can understand all that, but why is he in the care business and why is he my nominated carer.

Lots of things have changed, not least my mobility which is now dead slow and stop, I keep resisting the wheel chair on offer, screw them, I am not for being pushed around. Winston the little guttersnipe, helps me but in a vindictive way, he squeezes my arms, he pushes me in bed and drags me by the arms. I feel sometimes I could beat him with my walking stick, but I fear he'd kick me to death as a reprisal.

Winston the feral rat has been with me for four months now, I see very little of anyone else and I avoid the lounge where half the folk there stare listlessly at the gormless TV. Some of the girls are nice and Alex and co still parade at bedtime with my pills. I spend the days thinking about how I can thwart Winston, how I can mess him about. I'm not sure who is winning this all-consuming war. My hate for him festers by the day. He gets rougher every day, but I never say "You hurt me!" no I never let him know he has the upper hand.

I know Winston would like me to die, but fuck him, I'm not going to die any day soon.

At my monthly check up the pretty nurse with the blonde bob, notices my bruises, on my arms and on my side.

"John, how did you get these?" She gently dabs my side with a soft cotton swab.

"Fell down" My response in brief and sharp. None of her bloody business. Maybe it is her business, but the war with Winston is my business and nobody else's.

"John, I'm sorry but I have to call Alex."

"No, no it's fine please don't call any one please!." I smile my most charming smile, what's left of it.

"Hmph! Let's see to your leg and she soothes my gammy leg, a treat I look forward to every month."

"Hello, Winston, come in, we're nearly done, you can help Mr Betts to where ever." She smiles, I sneer at Winston, our war will continue.

By the afternoon McCann has called a meeting with me, Alex, the lovely nurse and Doctor Whatshisname. At first I refuse to be examined, I deny any wrong doing by Winston, I will win that battle on my own and in my own way.

How? I have no idea, but it's my job and that's
it.

Much to my disappointment Winston disappears,
fired I guess. No one says a word. My new
carer will start a soon as one is found. I am cross
that Winston got away with it, the nasty little
feral runt.

After two days of Alex fussing about me, Roddy
is brought to meet me. "Mr Betts, this is Roddy,
he's a student doing gap year and he wants to
work with us, and then go to medical school,
he's nineteen and comes from Swansea."

Roddy is slight, he wears the carers smock. He
has a kind face, narrow but sensitive. His hair is
mousy brown, he can't weigh more than ten
stone. I must try to be nice, the taste of Winston
is still strong in my nostrils.

"Hello Mr Betts," he offers his gentle hand .
"I'm sorry if I'm nervous, but I am." He looks
to the floor. I instantly decide to like him. He

tells me he's going to London Hospital to study medicine, but he would very much like to work with senior folk before that. He's a lovely gentle guy, the opposite of you know who.

Alex assures me that despite his very limited experience he will be backed up by Alex and others. Roddy patiently and I guess anxiously waits outside my door.

"Call him back in," Roddy appears diffidently at the door. "Come in Roddy and be my friend and keeper, we shall be pals." He beams a huge smile. Ah, resurrection. The thing is there are very few people here now that I know who are awake during the day. That includes me, by the way. Since HB died, I am aware that I have gone down-hill. Tomos disappearing was a big blow, and my battle with Winston the jackal was short lived. Despite the meanness of Winston, I enjoyed disliking him. Yes he pushed me around and even kicked me, I just enjoyed the shear focus of nastiness that existed between us.

I didn't have a battle plan, I didn't want Winston found out, I wanted to win, but I didn't know how. Anyway they caught the little shit and he's been fired. There is some comfort in that the institution, the nurse and Alex saved me from my self and Winston.

Roddy is a new partnership, I look forward to spending my awake time with him. He seems kind and gentle but also intelligent. Looking after me or the collective 'us' must be awful. So far at least I can wipe my own bum. My mobility is now awful I have to be pushed around in a wheel chair, I hate it, I am the now the most useless of my old pals. No pub outings, no cricket to look forward to just my weekly skype with David and his family. Dr. Dotty calls about once a month, the solicitor lady only comes if asked.

Dear old Brian, whispers and forgets a lot, Geoff still refers to his odd socks and we try to get together for a gentle scotch once a week.

369

I am barely aware of the time and season, I notice if is raining or snowing, which it did quite a lot earlier this year, I think it was this year. Roddy has settled in and reads me the times every morning. We debate the comment section and we enjoy a bit of a rip now and again. Roddy is really a sweet boy, and I'd love to meet his family.

McCann still tires to dragoon me into various group functions with people I don't know. I have no desire to know them, apart from which, I see very badly, hear very badly and move very badly all of which conspires to make me enjoy my own company and dear Roddy. Roddy is my carer six hours a day. He is tip top at the computer thingy and my conferences with David are now regular and quite jolly.

Brian has been ill again and down in the medical wing, don't know what the problem is but I must say he looks awful. I try to comfort him but I'm not so good at that either. I went down to see him this morning.

"Christ, Brian you look awful!"

Roddy tutu tutted, and gave me a gentle push. "Anyway.", I continued, "how long are the buggers keeping you in the lockup?" Brian whimpered a reply I didn't hear.

Roddy was chatting up the duty nurse, whilst I delivered a not very articulate monologue to dear old Brian. Looks to me as if it's all up for the dear old queen. It's only after I've returned to my room that I feel a bit sad. All my buddies are checking out. As the girls say, soon, soon.

I remember how I used to hate nothing, but now nothing seems harmless. Nothing is the precursor of sleep and I sleep a lot. Roddy always knows when I'm about to fall asleep, he makes my comfortable and he disappears only when I have dozed off.

It is spring time, and the weather looks wonderful through my window. I feel full of beans.

"Roddy let's go down to the garden, it's a lovely day." It really is and my leg seems not to hurt at all. We go via the lockup, I am coached to be kind to Brian who is still hanging on. Suddenly I remember Dan and wonder if I should stuff a pillow over Brian's head. I still don't have the guts. After a five minute whispering session, Roddy wheels me into the garden. It's so fresh

"Leave me here Roddy I'll take in the fresh air.
"You sure, Mr Betts?"

"Of course I'm sure." I sit, I am happy, the swallows are back.

About the Author:

Anthony James has been writing books for twenty years since his retirement from an international and extensively travelled career.

He lives in Wales with his lovely wife Dawn

His other books include the following:

Smiles in Africa

The Accidental Spy

The Poisoned Banquet

My Boy – A memoir

The psychedelic Traveller – short stories

The Winning Habit

Where the Swallows Fly

Printed in Great Britain
by Amazon

53791452R00225